*Dragon's*
CAPTIVE

A SCI-FI DRAGON SHIFTER ROMANCE
SHEA MALLOY

Copyright © 2020 Shea Malloy

All rights reserved.

This book or any portion thereof may not be reproduced or used in any manner whatsoever without the express permission of the publisher except for the use of brief quotations in a book review.

This book is a work of fiction. Any resemblance to persons, living or dead, or places, events or locations is purely coincidental. The characters are all productions of the author's imagination.

This book is intended only for adults 18 years of age or over.

Cover designed by Kasmit Covers

I liked it better when you didn't exist.
I liked it better when I didn't know that I needed you.

Chapter One

Seela

True thirst isn't just parched lips and a tongue that sticks to the roof of your mouth.

It's desperation, dizziness, and limbs made of lead.

It's discovering the sight of running water is as wonderful as the face of a loved one you haven't seen in a long time.

Dumping my bag of meager belongings on the river's edge, I hurl myself into the river with the dregs of energy I have left.

If any threats lurk within the bushes, this is the moment when I'm most defenseless. When my face is shoved so far into the water's depths that the tip of my nose almost scrapes the earthy bedding.

Dragon's Captive

Water sluices down my face as I rise up from the river and gasp for air. I don't have patience to sterilize the water and I don't care about its heavy, earthy taste. The cool water is heaven on my lips and tongue. Splashing my front, I drench my hot skin.

My pants squelch and dribble water when I sit down beside my bag. My stomach growls despite all the water I just drank, so I dig into my bag for the berry vine and nibble on the round, dark-blue fruit.

A cool breeze rustles the violet tree leaves. The air grows chillier as evening arrives. The sun has already set, but the last vestiges of light glimmer on the river's surface.

It's the first source of drinkable water I've found in days. This dense forest is filled with swamps, insects, and animals of various species that don't take kindly to a human tromping through their territory.

It's easy to learn about the geography of where you live from the safety of a console or from someone else. It's definitely not as easy acquiring the knowledge from firsthand experience.

Ikkon's laughter, roughened by age, echoes in my head, his bronze eyes lit with amusement in his lined face.

You are not as tough as you think, Seela, he would tease if he were here.

An invisible grip wraps around my heart and squeezes. I blink rapidly to hold back the tears of loss and rage. Lost in the belly of an Andrasari forest, it's hard to accept that the one constant in my life is gone. They took him from me. My home is gone too. All I have left is the will to find somewhere else to live.

Another passing breeze carries the sound of people screaming. The terror and panic inflected in it makes me anxious. It reminds me too much of what I went through before finding this forest.

Slinging my bag over my shoulder, I lurch to my feet. A roar overpowers the screams. The reverberant sound of trees splitting and tumbling to the floor shakes the ground.

Birds squawk and shoot toward the lavender sky. My heart rate escalates, the thumps like drums in my chest.

Rur draki.

Run away.

The warning's urgency intensifies when the screaming stops. In the growing dark, the silence is eerie and foreboding. Yet, I'm curious.

Against good judgement, I make my way to where I'd heard the screaming. Ikkon said to me once that my curiosity was a gift from the mother of fire and goddess of planet Rur, Kahafura. He also said that if I wasn't careful, it would be my downfall.

Maybe this is why us humans are slaves to the *draki*. We ignored logic in favour of discovery.

Why are you doing this?

There might be survivors and they might need my help.

When Ikkon needed me, I couldn't do anything to save him. But maybe I can help these people. Although, I'm not sure what I can do for any unfortunate soul that fights a dragon. Maybe the assistance I'll offer is ending their suffering with my blade in their neck.

My steps are light, my shoulders hunched. Thick, maroon bushes high as my shoulders graze my skin. The stench of burnt flesh and smoke permeates the heated air, my skin dampening with sweat.

Crouching low, I part the bushes. A small clearing has been made from felled trees. Some of them are on fire. Amid the burning trees lay a black mountain of hard, powerful flesh. Its wings lay at rest, though curled close to its body because the area is cramped.

Blades protrude from its body, the obsidian gleam marking them as Rurium steel.

Charred, human-shaped lumps are scattered around the dragon. Did the dragon attack the humans or did the humans strike first?

While the story of how humans came to live on Rur has been embellished for entertainment, we still know the truth.

In Earth *enu* 2237, our planet became inhospitable due to extreme levels of radiation. Only a handful managed escape via spaceship.

The remnants of our species scoured space for another habitable planet until an accidental fall through a wormhole led us to Rur.

Humans were given refuge within one of Rur's regions called Andrasar by its *Konai*—High Prince—Dohar Visclaud. One year later, Dohar died and his brother, Aphat Visclaud, became the Konai.

Aphat's first edict as the new Konai of Andrasar: enslave the humans.

For twenty-eight years, humans have endured enslavement by the Andrasari with nary a resistance. Until now. There are reports of rebellions, of humans fighting against the Andrasari. Humans banding together to push back against slavery.

In their primary form, the Rur beings can almost pass for humans. Except for their eyes that gleam with the fire trapped in their bellies.

They are formidable when they morph into their dragon form. It's a fool's errand to fight against a *draki*. The dead humans laying there learned this the hard way.

Leave. Now. It's a must if I want to live. But I'm transfixed by the dragon. A beautiful monstrosity that terrifies me from the top of my head to the tips of my toes.

I'm in awe of how much strength is encased in that huge beast. It must be so freeing to be so powerful. To know that everyone and everything quivers in your mighty presence.

The dragon's eyes are closed. Is it dead? Light plumes of smoke drifts from its snout which means it's breathing. Maybe I should help it. Go out there and offer to remove the blades from its body so it can heal properly.

Don't be stupid, Seela. You'll be its next victim.

Ikkon's words resonate in my head.

Every life has value.

But what about the life of my people's murderer? Only a few Andrasari have ever been kind to me, Ikkon chief among them. The others consider my kind the enemy. They enslave us, torture us, kill us.

Dead humans surround the dragon.

Humans it burned alive.

Shouldn't it die too?

My heart thuds in my chest, my mouth dry from the oppressive heat. My sodden clothing clings to my skin, heavy and uncomfortable.

Every bit of me says I should flee, yet I'm held captive by some inexplicable bind. It's as if Kahafura led me here for a purpose and demands I see it through.

The dragon lifts its head abruptly and opens its eyes. It swivels its head, and its twin magnificent golden orbs tinged with vermilion pins me where I crouch.

My heart grounds to a stop then restarts at a pace that leaves me struggling to breathe. Rising from my crouch onto shaking legs, I hold my empty hands high and visible.

Then I step free from my hiding spot with an echoing squish from my shoes.

I speak quickly, my voice clawing its way out of my chest. "I can help you."

That day I lost Ikkon, when I was forced to leave my home was terrifying. This moment, staring into the fiery depths of the eyes of a *draki*, is comparable.

Lifting its wings, the dragon climbs to its clawed feet, reinforcing its massive size, its strength, its capabilities despite its injuries. I'm an idiot for letting it discover me and I'm going to pay the price for my stupidity.

The dragon advances, its left wing lower than the right, each stomp vibrating the ground. I take a few steps in retreat.

Is running away too late for me? Absolutely. I'll be burnt to a crisp the moment I turn my back to this monster. So, I remain still and face my approaching doom.

Except, my approaching doom buckles and falls to the ground before it reaches me.

It roars, the awful sound whipping my heart into a frenzy. Rows of long, sharp, ivory teeth designed to crush bone with a single bite, and the brilliant orange blooming from the dark cavern of its mouth make my skin tighten.

"I can help you," I say again, raising my hands higher. "I can remove the blades."

My voice breaks on the words. I'm going to die. After running the race of survival in this forest, this is my finish line.

A low, rumbling sound escapes the dragon. It closes its mouth and its wings deflate. But its brilliant golden eyes are fixed on me.

Watching.

Waiting.

This is my moment to flee, isn't it? So why don't I? Why do I step forward instead even though my legs threaten to give out from under me? Why do I take another step?

It's absurd, but I have this sense that I was meant to save this dark behemoth. But the closer I get to it, the harder I shake.

I'm the foolish prey sacrificing itself willingly to its predator.

There's a burnt body beside my feet, the ground scorched black beneath it, but I maintain eye contact with the dragon to prove my sincerity.

I'm close enough for it to turn me into nothing but ash, close enough for it to rise up and gobble me whole.

Chapter Two

Seela

Ikkon never showed me his dragon form, so this is the first time I've been this close to one.

I can't help admiring it. The spiralling gold and the black slits in its eyes fascinate me.

There are ridges on its head and symmetrical half-circle patterns on its flesh. Its wings alone dwarf me and strengthen my sense of insignificance.

I wait for a sign that it accepts my offer. It hasn't killed me yet so I guess that's a positive. If I live past today, this'll be a great story to tell.

I, Seela Pith, faced a rur draki. *Here I am, alive and whole, to share this remarkable tale.*

The dragon thumps its tail once, its intense gaze never wavering.

My steps are tentative. Any sudden movements and I'm done. This moment is so surreal. It's like I'm apart from myself, watching myself commit an act that's unquantifiable levels of idiotic.

Standing close, the dragon's warmth bathes my skin, its scent like fresh earth. It curves its neck to watch me while I inspect the first blade embedded in its left shoulder.

The lone injury would've killed a human, yet the dragon still stands with these blades impaled in its body.

Removing the blades seems ill-advised but I have no choice. Ikkon said that a Rur being has healing properties in its blood. In order for it to work, I'm certain these foreign objects have to leave its body first.

When I gingerly pull the first blade free, dark blood geysers from the wound. Blood dribbling free, the opening doesn't close like I'd expected it to. I worry my plan might not work.

"I will have to climb on top of you to remove the others," I say, forging ahead. I don't know how I manage the words when the thought makes me want to vomit the berries I ate.

It's torture waiting for it to accept what I'm about to do. There's a long silence when I'm sure it'll kill me for even suggesting I climb it like if it's a common animal.

The dragon thumps its tail again.

Thankfully, the rest of its body doesn't have ridges like those on its head. I climb onto its back and I swear to the goddess my heart might explode.

Its flesh is warm, rough and textured. But as much as I want to savour this experience of being atop a dragon, I'm aware there are consequences for dawdling.

The dragon regards me over its shoulder and I can sense its distrust even though it has allowed me to come this far.

The dragon shivers with pain with each blade I pull free, its blood spilling from the open wounds. Was this the right choice? I'm not a medic. I am—was—a simple baker's assistant. What if it dies from blood loss?

There's one more blade buried in the joint where its wing meets its body. This is why the wing hung lower than the other. Why the dragon didn't fly away after the attack.

When my fingers touch the blade's hilt, the dragon growls at me, its eyes flashing with anger. My heart gallops and I rear back.

"You can't fly if it's there."

Making sure our gazes remain connected, my movement slow and deliberate, I free the blade.

The dragon roars and bucks, pitching me from its back. A grunt escapes me when my body hits the ground hard. Pain blossoms in the side of my head and spreads throughout my body.

Temporarily winded from the fall, my chest is tight. My body demands air. I gasp and roll onto my back. Despite the pain, I can appreciate the irony of my situation.

In an effort to help my enemy, I hurt myself.

The dragon stomps toward me, looms over me, its fearsome visage blocking out everything else in sight.

If this beast wants to kill me, so be it. I deserve it for being so stupid. What's the point of fighting to live in this world when there's no-one left who wants me?

Its eyes are like twin torches, scorching me with its gaze.

Cold acceptance envelops me.

I wait for it to take my life.

But the dragon recedes. Not just away from me, but in size. Its towering frame morphs and diminishes into a male Andrasari in his primary form. His golden eyes shimmer before they're shuttered away behind closed lids, and he sinks to the floor.

My life is spared.

Unaware of my own movement, I sit up and push to my feet. I wipe away the tears I didn't know I cried from my face and hesitate drawing closer to the prone Andrasari male.

I've helped him as much as I can, right? I'm sure he's able to heal on his own from here. I played the game of chance with my life and yet, somehow, I'm the winner.

Wouldn't it be foolish to play another turn?

Ikkon once said that what I should fear above everything else was the consequences of selfish actions and how they might hurt others. That I should help when it was within my power to do so, because to turn someone away in their worst moments invited unrelenting guilt in my chest.

And you wouldn't want to live with that feeling, Seela. It gives you terrible indigestion!

So, I approach the prone Andrasari and kneel beside him.

Darkness creeps in as evening cedes to night. The bit of light from the dying fire fades.

It's not the first time I've seen a naked male—my lone encounter with an Andrasari farmer's slave in a barn made sure of that—but I've never seen such visible strength encased in a body like this.

His flesh is bronze, his ribcage and upper arms covered in a network of golden half-circles. Scars mark his flesh too. His abdomen is grooved and defined from years of physical activity, his upper arms and thighs powerful muscle.

I intentionally avoid looking at that part between his legs. Warmth suffuses my face and the tips of my ears. The gash on his left shoulder is closed but it's an angry red against his bronze skin.

Grabbing his arms, I intended to roll him onto his front so I could inspect the wounds on his back when my gaze shifts to his face.

Whatever breath I had left over from the smoke disappears.

His eyes are open, capturing mine. In that moment, it's as if we are connected by more than just our stare. Warmth coils in the pit of my stomach like the beginnings of arousal. Surprise briefly flickers in his eyes before it's replaced by fury.

I recognize his face.

I know who he is.

Nai Theron Visclaud, the Konai's nephew.

He is the Overseer of Andrasar. The one who enforces the enslavement and perpetual misery of humans.

My initial thought is to flee, but horror immobilizes me. He lurches up onto his feet in one fluid motion leaving me on my knees before him. His gaze is like an unseen hand, lifting my chin so that my attention is focused solely on him.

"Were you a part of this group, human?" His voice is silken, his eyes gleaming with hatred.

I swallow, willing words to my lips.

"I wasn't. I travel alone."

He amber gaze bores into me and searches my soul. I guess he's seen me for what I am, a scared human who poses no threat to him, because he smiles. It's not warm or friendly. It's sinister in its triumphant curving of his lips.

"If you had known my identity would you have helped me?" When I attempt to stand, he points at me with fingers lengthened into claws. "Stay where you are and answer the question."

Tense silence hangs between us. Would I have been a traitor to humans by saving the life of our oppressor? With Theron Visclaud gone, the rebellion would be strengthened considerably.

Freedom from slavery would no longer be a distant hope, but a possibility. The courage to fight for a positive change would surpass the fear of consequence.

Would I have knowingly crushed this opportunity?

But I was taught to cherish life. *Every life has value* was Ikkon's belief, and to an extent, I adopted it too.

It didn't matter that our species were enemies, Ikkon took me into his home and raised me like his own daughter when I lost my family as a baby. Through his example, I've always sought to show a similar kindness to others.

My gaze level with the Andrasari's chest, I speak softly. "Some humans believe in a spiritual principle called..." There's no translation for the word in Rur language, so I speak it in Human Standard. "...karma. It means both good and bad deeds are rewarded, whether in your current life or in a reincarnated life. Good actions reward you with happiness and bad actions reward you with suffering."

Darkness cloaks us like if we're a secret it must hide. The moonlight and last bit of fire still awards enough light for me to see his face.

He remains silent, his features indecipherable.

"I believe in karma, too. I would still have helped even if I had known who you were. Saving your life prolongs the suffering of humans in the present, but maybe this good action might bring about future happiness for my people."

Chapter Three

Theron

Humans may resemble a Rur being when we are in our primary form, but they are nothing like us.

They are weak and cowardly. Dishonourable. I have read their books Aphat confiscated from their spaceship several enur ago. In those books are their history, and it is rife with selfishness, greed, and destruction of their own kind.

They do not belong on this planet, let alone in my home region, Andrasar.

The great Kahafura took my *kaha* and *toha*'s life for blighting us with the presence of these foreign creatures. In retribution for my parents' death I have facilitated their misery. Yet, they continue to survive and grow in numbers.

Ambushed by a group of humans who almost took my life, I found immense satisfaction in taking theirs.

But kneeling before me is another human. The female with skin the colour of desert sand, her hair as wild and curling as tree vines, her eyes as dark as the night surrounding us, their depths filled with unsettling sincerity.

She saved my life. She boldly approached me in my dragon form. Risked her safety to remove the blades from my body. Admits that despite what I've done to her kind, she would save my life again if given the chance.

This human is not weak or cowardly or selfish, but an anomaly that contradicts my long-held beliefs of her species.

She is also the one my dragon claims as my *asafura*. My fire's half.

There must be a mistake. She is not a Rur being. How can she be my *asafura* if she does not possess fire inside her?

Yet my dragon insists she is mine. Heat builds in my stomach the longer I look at her. I fight against the arousal and my dragon's demand that I push her to the floor and take her.

"You are foolish," I say, outraged by my treacherous thoughts. "As long as I am alive, your worthless species will never find happiness."

Her eyebrows draw closer together, her eyes narrowing. "You're the one who's foolish. Holding on to so much hate for beings you consider inferior only makes you weaker than them."

Her insult will not be tolerated regardless of what my dragon says she is to me. I lunge for her, grabbing the front of her shirt. She withdraws a Rurium blade from the waist of her trousers and points it at me. Her eyes are alight with a similar fury residing in me.

"Just because I saved your life and said all that shit about karma doesn't mean I'll hesitate to hurt you, you ungrateful bastard."

I sneer at her. "You'll never succeed. I'll rip that insolent tongue out of your head first before I take your life."

"Maybe you're right, but I'm willing to try."

The blade surges forward and I shove her away. Her body barely touches the ground before she's on her feet, sprinting away from me through the trees.

I chase her despite the pain from my injuries and grab her before she can get far. With angry snarls, she fights me and manages to stab my arm twice with the blade's edge.

Stinging heat surrounds where the blade penetrated and I hiss. Holding her wrists, I shove her body against a tree trunk and squeeze her wrists until she cries out. The blood-covered blade slips from her fingers to the grassy floor with a dull thump.

Pressing my front to hers, I use my weight and strength to prevent her from kneeing me or squirming free. The poison that coated the blades from my earlier attack weaken me, but I am still much stronger than her.

Belatedly, I realize this is far too intimate a position to be in with a human. Especially the one who Kahafura has incorrectly chosen as mine.

Her heat seeps into my flesh and she pants from her struggle, her breasts rising and falling against my chest. The fire has died, but moonlight softens the darkness. Her eyes glitter with anger and dislike.

Our faces are close.

Too close.

It is forbidden for an Andrasari to lay with a human. But it isn't unheard of that some have broken this rule. To lay with a human is unnatural. I have never considered any of them attractive because to do so would be to see them as an equal and worthy of my attention.

Yet once again, this human female is the exception. My reaction an aberration. She smells like the forest and mild sweat. Every being's unique scent is reminiscent of their personality and hers is gentle but edged with determination.

Her warm breath fans my skin forcing my gaze to her lips. A foreign voice in my head whispers a question that disturbs me.

What do her lips taste like?

"Why don't you get it over with already?" she demands, which disturbs me even further because it's as if she's asking me to actualize my sick thoughts about kissing her.

No, she wants me to hasten her death. She struggles to project fearlessness but the scent of her terror fills the air between us. And just beneath that terror is the wisps of lust.

This human female desires me.

The urge to take her, to rip her clothing from her, to press my face between her legs and inhale her overcomes me stronger than before. I release her as if her flesh has become scalding, as if touching her is the reason this new demon inhabits my body.

My wings unfurl from my back as I shift into my dragon. She remains where she stands pressed against the tree trunk, her eyes wide as she regards the beast before her.

What a shame. This is her lone chance to run, to escape, to save herself from the wrath that is me.

Dragon's Captive

When she does, it's too late.

"No!" she says in alarm as I grasp her and take flight.

She screams. Her useless noises die when we are airborne, and she trembles.

She hugs my claws tight to her body as if it will prevent me from releasing her and letting her plummet to her death. Even though the wind tries to steal her voice, I hear her pleas that I put her down and let her go. I ignore her.

Most Andrasari prefer to fly in the day when the sun's heat is at its strongest. In the warmer seasons, festivals are held celebrating the high temperatures as a blessing from Kahafura. There are ice-covered mountains in Andrasar, but we rarely endure freezing temperatures. Unlike the region, Seca, the land of perpetual ice and cold.

I like to fly at night. The cool wind buffeting my wings, pressing against my face, and gliding along my scales. At night, it's quiet and peaceful, the sky an endless stretch of indigo speckled with light.

When I was younger, my *kaha* would say that those speckles were the souls of dead loved ones. They were preserved by Kahafura to spare us from the despair of losing someone you loved.

Perhaps this is why I favour flying at night. It's my only chance to be close to her and *toha* after all these years.

The glittering city lights speed toward us. In the center, is the Andrak's towering spire. I maintain altitude above the marked path of speeding air cruisers, my reflection a dark ghost on the sides of glass buildings.

Landing in the Andrak's courtyard, I release the human and shift into my primary form. Guards approach us with querying looks and the human female sidles close to me before she remembers that I am an enemy too.

She lurches away, her shoulders hunched, her arms away from her body in a defensive posture. Her widened eyes dart about her surroundings in fear.

"Why am I here?"

No longer secluded in the dark forest, I can assess her fully. She is not dressed as a *zevyet* should be and her neck is devoid of a collar of ownership. How did she remove it without her master's authorization?

"To be imprisoned for your crimes."

"What crimes?" she spits, glaring. Her fear evaporates. She is a perfect ball of indignation.

"You have abandoned your duties to your *zevyena* and you wilfully attacked a member of the Konai's service."

"I am not a slave. I've never had a master to abandon."

She's never had a master? Impossible. All humans are either property of an Andrasari or work as a slave in whatever capacity that serves Andrasar.

"Take her to the cells," I order the guards.

I don't derive the usual satisfaction from panic twisting a human's features. An unpleasant feeling nags at me. My dragon bristles when the guards seize her arms.

No-one else should touch her but me.

"I didn't have a master, I had a guardian," she says, tears brimming in her eyes as she fights against the guards dragging her away. "And I didn't abandon him. He was murdered."

Chapter Four

Theron

The moment the human disappears with the guards, the tension in my body eases and my mind clears.

It's unacceptable how much of my attention her presence consumed. As I stand in the courtyard, I question my sanity for bringing her to the Andrak.

The charges I've laid against her are punishable by death—which I could have executed in the forest without this much fuss.

But if it's true that she is my *asafura*, I can't kill her.

So what am I to do with her? I don't want nor can I have a human as my mate.

Forcing my thoughts away from the human and her parting words, I make my way up to my home.

As I shower, I ponder on my attack. Earlier today, I was approached by a human notifying me that Ronan wanted to meet in the forest to 'discuss a private matter'. However, Ronan never showed.

Instead, a group armed with Rurium blades coated in poison attacked me. Those weapons aren't easily procured by humans. When the group encountered me, they hadn't seemed surprised by my presence. They charged at me like soldiers given an order.

An order given by who? It certainly wasn't Ronan. General Ronan Coya is like family to me. He was my *toha*'s closest friend and grieved his death like a brother. The years of pain and misery I've endured in my childhood beneath Aphat's hand would have been worse without Ronan's protection.

Someone wants me dead. No doubt, the humans. To think they almost succeeded. I have been taking the rebellions too lightly, it seems. Complacent in the knowledge that their silly, haphazard revolts will be crushed beneath the heel of Andrasari's strength.

Perhaps they have acquired a leader. An intelligent one with access to dangerous weapons.

My vision blurs as I dress. I become dizzy. Blinking rapidly, I sink onto my bed. Sudden weariness turns my limbs to lead. I had a lengthy shift in my dragon form and I have not eaten in some time. My body still heals from the attack and battles the poison.

My movement is sluggish as I touch the small metal circle of my communication implant just behind my right ear.

"Theron, where have you been all day?" Eyin asks as soon as her holographic image blooms in front of me. She furrows her eyebrows, her amber eyes filled with concern. "You look unwell."

"Poison," I say. "I am in my quarters."

"I'll be there shortly."

Eyin disconnects and I lay back on the bed, the sheets cool against my skin.

My eyes drift shut and the human female's face fills the darkness behind my closed eyelids.

I was ready to burn her alive the instant she stepped out of hiding. Her courage despite her visible terror intrigued me. She spoke to me honestly. The first of her kind to challenge me and live to see another day.

How could such a dynamic presence be contained in a small creature like her? There is a long-standing joke that Kahafura's humour is dark and filled with incredible ironies.

It's not a joke anymore. Not for me.

Finding one's *asafura* is rare and an occasion that merits celebration. Yet I can't enjoy this moment when a union with a human is verboten.

The door to my living area opens and slides shut. Eyin's footsteps pad toward my bedroom. I'm thankful for the distraction from thoughts of the human.

"Are you dead already?" she asks, her voice light.

"I am within reach of the goddess' embrace."

Opening my eyes, I find concern lurking in Eyin's features.

Her long, dark hair is tied up into a hasty bun as usual. A few strands hang loosely over the left side of her face to cover the scar that lives there.

My *rahsa* is beautiful but she doesn't believe this. She only hears the whispers behind her back that her scar is ugly. So she hides behind her hair and her work as a medic within the Andrak.

"Stop staring at me like that," she orders, fidgeting.

She doesn't like when I stare at her scar. She thinks I look at her with pity. It isn't pity, it's disappointment in myself that I wasn't able to protect her from Aphat's cruelty.

"You shouldn't hide it, Eyin," I say, sitting up. I try to brush the hair back from her face but she swats my hand away. "You should let him see it and be reminded of what he's done."

"But it only reminds you, Theron. You know he hasn't a remorseful bone in his body." She sets down her kit of medical supplies on the bed beside me. "Now enough of that. How were you poisoned?"

I remove my shirt and show her the healing injuries on my back.

Her touch is gentle as she traces the tender spots. She doesn't touch the older scars but I know she looks at them too.

"These are stab wounds," she says, her voice harsh with anger. "Who did this to you?"

Several seconds pass as I decide how much I am willing to share with her. Eyin is one of my closest friends. When our parents died, it felt as if the whole of Andrasar had turned against us. All we had, all we could depend on, was each other.

We try not to hide things from each other, but there are things I've seen and done that I will never disclose to Eyin. Certainly, there are secrets she has never shared with me, too.

Some truths are best left unspoken if it means protecting those you love from rash decisions. Eyin is a calm, intelligent being, but she is prone to wilful actions regardless of consequences.

She has a vengeful nature. If I tell Eyin my attack seemed to be premeditated, Eyin will not be as patient as me in her quest for revenge—no matter her views on humans.

"I was attacked by humans in my dragon form."

She frowns, but makes no comment. She produces a portable medical scanner, the blue light illuminating my skin as she assesses me.

"The poison is slowing the process, but the muscle and bone damage are almost fully repaired," Eyin says, eyeing the scanner's screen. "The skin is healing, too. Unfortunately, I don't think your *Shifted* blood is going to protect you from scarring this time." Setting down the scanner, she hands me a container. "Hold this. You're going to need it soon."

Retrieving a syringe from her kit, Eyin withdraws blood from me and tests it. After reading the results, she fills another syringe with a clear solution.

She pokes my flesh with the syringe's point and queasiness attacks the moment the solution is entirely administered. I cough up the contents of my stomach into the container she handed me.

"Unpleasant side-effect of the antidote," she says with a sympathetic grimace as she pats my shoulder. She hands me a cloth to wipe my mouth. Her features become serious, her voice soft. "Was the attack unprovoked, Theron?"

I scowl. "Yes."

"Are you telling the truth?"

"It was unprovoked," I insist. "I went for a flight and when I landed, I was ambushed by a group of them." I shrug. "Perhaps I startled them or disrupted one of their rebel meetings."

The corners of her mouth turn down in disapproval.

"You killed them."

It's not a question. She knows my views on humans. But Eyin does not share my belief that humans don't belong in Andrasar.

She doesn't blame them for our family's demise like I do. She has this preposterous idea that humans and Rur beings can live together in peaceful, equal harmony.

I have cautioned her to never speak these thoughts aloud if she values her life.

"Of course I killed them," I say. My scowl deepens that my tone is defensive. "They tried to kill me. Should I have let them? Would you rather a group of animals who murdered your brother alive and standing?"

"They aren't the animals, Theron," she says quietly as she packs away her medical supplies. She faces me. "You are. You all are. You, Ronan, and Aphat."

The disappointment shining in her amber gaze is like one of those Rurium blades to my chest. Likening me to Ronan, I don't mind, but for her to see me on par with Aphat only adds extreme insult to injury.

"I am not like Aphat," I say coldly. "Aphat nor Ronan wouldn't have spared the life of a human who harmed them but I did."

I recount the tale of the human female appearing and removing the blades, our disagreement that led to our brief scuffle and her stabbing me. I make no mention that she is my *asafura*.

Eyin frowns. "She saved your life and you repay her by imprisoning her?"

"Preserving her life is repayment enough."

"You are better than this, Theron." She shakes her head. "You can do better than this."

Her disappointment does not abate. I dislike that she makes me feel like a child who has done something terrible. This is not the first time we've been at odds over my treatment of humans, but there's something about this instance that bothers me.

I don't want to admit it to her or to myself, but she

is right. As much as it galls me, every breath I take henceforth is courtesy of the human's efforts. Imprisoning her was a dishonourable act.

"There is nothing else for me to do with her," I say. "She has a stubborn nature. If I put her to work in the Andrak, she will foolishly attempt escape and be killed when she's discovered."

Eyin's eyes are lit with excitement. "Well, since she was quick to help and smart enough to know what to do, she might not mind staying if she works in the infirmary. I can train her as my assistant."

"Absolutely not. Humans can't be trusted, especially in these times when they plot rebellions against us. I will not put your life in jeopardy."

"If you freed them, viewed them as equals worthy of respect and rights then they wouldn't need to plot rebellions." She purses her lips. "You don't always have to be my protector, Theron. I can handle myself just fine."

Scowling, I don't respond to her first statement.

"I will always be your protector as long as the goddess gives me breath." An idea forms as I don my shirt. I don't relish it, but it's a temporary solution that might benefit me in the fight against the rebels. "The human will no longer be imprisoned. I have decided what I will do with her."

Chapter Five

Seela

After living in the forest, prison's like a vacation.

In the forest, I made my bed on the hard, earthen floor or against a rough tree trunk. The temperature vacillated between sweltering in the day, and chilly in the night.

Food had to be either caught and wrestled into submission or carefully chosen in case they were poisonous. Water was sparse.

Then there were the creatures that wanted me dead on sight and chased after me with single-minded rage. The insects that pecked at my skin or liked to crawl into my mouth or my clothing as I slept.

Worst of all was the darkness. The moonless nights that blanketed the forest in a shroud so thick,

Dragon's Captive

I couldn't see my fingers even when I held them right up to my eyes.

Prison, on the other hand, is a rectangle ablaze with light. Three sides of thick, transparent glass, the fourth side reinforced metal.

I have a chair, a table, and a diminutive toilet. The bed isn't much, but a thin piece of foam on a slab elevated from the ground is superior to an upraised, gnarly tree root for a pillow.

They took my bag that held my time-piece so I don't know how much time has passed. I slept, but it was fitful and now I'm more tired than before. What I would love is a shower that's not a quick splash in a river.

What I would love most of all is my freedom.

But the guards beyond the glass regarding me with dead eyes in their granite faces is proof that the latter is beyond my reach.

So I sit at the table with my arms crossed and I wait.

Wait for what?

A part of me still believes I'll find justice. I've been imprisoned for crimes I didn't commit. Is it a crime if I hurt someone in self-defense? These finer points don't matter because of what I am and who I hurt, I guess. A human wielding a weapon against a common Andrasari suffered vigorous beatings.

However, I stabbed *Nai* Theron Visclaud. If his father hadn't died when he was too young to assume rule, Theron would've been the Konai of Andrasar. As a prince, and as the Overseer, he is an important and respected being in Andrasar.

What's going to happen to me for hurting someone like him?

Anxiety seizes control of my limbs and makes me jittery. I'm on my feet, pacing the room as my indignation climbs.

This is so unfair. I saved that bastard's life and this is how he repays me? The next time I see him, I'll do more than a stab in his arm. My attack will be sure so that I'll truly earn my place in this prison.

As if the goddess has heard my violent promise and has decided to test my sincerity, the door leading to the prison cells slides open and Theron steps through.

Frozen in place, I watch him approach. My heart thuds harder in my chest and louder in my ears with each step that draws him closer. He stands outside the glass, facing me directly and I can't look away.

He wears a black jacket that accentuates his broad shoulders and fits his frame, as well as black pants and boots. A golden pin in the shape of dragon mid-flight is secured to his jacket over his right breast. His jaw is sharp angles softened by a dusting of dark hair against his bronze skin.

In the light, his eyes are bright gold.

In the light, he's incredibly, undeniably handsome.

Maybe it's this realization that steals all the air from my lungs. Or that he's opened the door to my prison cell and has stepped inside, his presence like a vacuum sucking up all of my oxygen.

Whatever angry words I had for him ready on the tip of my tongue abandons me. If I didn't feel like a traitor for saving his life, I certainly feel like one now for considering him attractive.

He studies me, not saying a word. I fidget beneath his blatant staring. What is he thinking? I restrain myself from a sudden stupid urge to fix my hair. On better days, my curls are pretty and manageable, but sometimes Ikkon used to tease that I was a walking bird's nest.

Finally, he speaks.

"What is your name, human?"

I hide my surprise. Most Andrasari don't bother to learn a human's name.

"Seela."

"And the name of your master?"

"He wasn't my—"

"When I ask you a question, I want you to answer it." He advances, his eyes glinting dangerously. "Never make me repeat myself or you will not like the consequences."

"Ikkon," I say, resisting the urge to retort. "He owned a bakery and I was his assistant."

"Until the day you murdered him."

Rising anger and hurt forces me back as if to escape his awful accusation.

"He was all I had. I would never hurt him."

His features harden. "Were you his lover too?"

"No," I say, disgusted by his question. "He was like a father to me."

He says nothing for a moment before he continues with his interrogation.

"Did you report his death?"

"I couldn't. I was pursued by his attackers until I fell into a swamp that covered my scent."

"Where did you live prior to your abandonment?"

Even though I know he's intentionally trying to rile me up, his words hurt because they're true. I should have stayed to help Ikkon, I should have ignored his plea that I run, and instead fought to protect him.

"Yoah."

"You were a long way from Yoah when we met. Where were you going?"

Unwilling to tell him the truth, I hesitate.

"The city. I guess I've arrived at my destination thanks to you."

Big mistake. I don't know how, but he knows I'm lying. He violates my personal space forcing me to retreat hastily. The table's edge jabs my hip, but I don't focus on the sting. My attention is gripped by this Andrasari male.

"Do you know what I do to liars, human?"

"Let me guess—you kill them?"

It's really the absolute worst time for sarcasm, but the words slip from my mouth before I can stop them. My eyes widen in shock that I spoke to him like that and the surprise replicates in his eyes too until he recovers.

"Yes, I kill them," he says. "There's nothing that satisfies me as much as giving someone who speaks untruths what they deserve." He leans in, his heat radiating onto me, his voice a caress as if he's my lover saying sweet things in my ear. "I start with their feet first. Why should a liar stand sure when their words are built on false foundations? Then I sever their fingers one at a time. A liar should not have use of their hands to commit acts of treachery. I take their tongue because it's fair that I take away their weapon. Their screams as my claws sink into their chest is not only a beautiful sound, it's transcendent."

His words have their desired effect. I have done courageous things, but I am not brave enough for this monster. My body trembles as much as it did when I first encountered him in dragon form.

"So, I'm going to ask you again, Seela," he speaks my name like if it's an insult, "and you are going to tell me the truth. From here on, you will always tell me the truth. Where were you going?"

"I was going to Tarro." I hate myself that I'm unable to face him when I speak, like if I'm some weak slave who fears her master.

"Humans aren't permitted to leave Andrasar. You would've been killed in your attempt."

"I was still going to try." The pit of my stomach tightens when I raise my gaze from the gleaming floor to look at him. Whatever that sensation means or represents, I don't know and I don't want to know. "I've heard the Rur beings in the Tarro region accepts everyone and enslaves no-one. I was willing to risk my life to see if a place like that really existed." I pause. "Instead, I risked my life to save you."

His stern mask cracks for a fleeting second. I would've missed it if my gaze had wavered a little bit. I'd like to think that minute break in his towering wall of hatred was guilt, but I guess if you look hard enough for something, you end up seeing it even if it's not there.

One thing I've learned for certain is that Theron Visclaud is exceptional at hiding his emotions.

"Then you'll be pleased I'm here to repay you for your efforts."

Amazed, I perk up with hope.

"Are you going to free me?"

"Yes," he says, and my heart soars. I can't believe it. He's letting me go free. Maybe I misjudged him. Maybe he's not a heartless bastard after all.

"Thank you," I say, my voice thick with relief.

And then he produces a silver, metal ring. There's a dull shine on its coat from the lights above us. I recognize what it is when he pries the ring apart. All the relief that made my heart airborne vanishes.

I plummet toward cruel reality. For the first time in my life, a *zevyet*'s collar is clamped around my throat.

Theron's golden eyes shine with satisfaction.

"You're welcome."

Chapter Six

Seela

Theron freed me from prison only to imprison me again as a slave.

But not for long.

He orders me to follow him as we leave the cell. As soon we go pass the prison's doors out into a corridor, I make a run for it.

In the back of my mind, I already anticipated I wouldn't get far. So, of course, I don't. With true belief, a person's hope is made real. Negativity, however, awards me a stinging zap from the collar.

My feet buckle and my body slumps to the floor. Mild heat spreads through me and a prickling sensation runs along my arms.

Theron stalks toward me, his features emotionless.

"Your collar is connected to my communication implant," he says, looming over me. "I can punish you with just a thought. I'm pleased you learned the consequences of disobeying me early."

I use the wall as support to stand. My dislike for him climbing higher.

"If this is how you treat someone who wanted to see you live, I shudder to think what you do to your enemies."

"You are my enemy. That spiritual guidance you call karma applies here. I will reward your bad behaviour with suffering."

I glare. "And if I'm good, how will you reward me?"

It's only after the words hang in the silence do I realize they sound like an inappropriate insinuation. His nostrils flare as if he understands this too. There's not much space between us, and the quiet creates an intimacy that shouldn't exist.

His gaze dips to my mouth and lingers there as if in consideration. I stand perfectly still, rigid with shock. There's no way he's entertaining that thought. Why would he want to kiss me after proclaiming me his enemy?

Why would I want this bastard to kiss me after what he's done?

"With the life in your body so you can continue to serve me."

His stare is harder and colder than ever before, his fingers like metal bands around my arm as he marches me forward. He jerks his hand away as if touching me is lethal to his health, but the heat of his touch remains on my skin.

The corridor walls are an unvarying grey with no windows, and the ceiling is low. There's a chill in the air and a musty odour that completes the dreariness of our surroundings. We must be underground.

Theron walks alongside me, his body held so straight I'm sure the back of his head aligns perfectly with his heels. He stares forward with a permanent glower.

"Where are you taking me?"

He doesn't respond. He doesn't acknowledge he's heard me speak. Typical Andrasari treatment of humans. Our species are insignificant to them and therefore our voices go unheard.

But no matter the consequences, I will not let him treat me like that.

"I exist," I say bitterly. "You can see me and hear me, just as I can see you and hear you."

"You exist only to serve your *zevyena*."

"The only master I will ever serve is myself."

I wait for him to zap me, or threaten me with death, or go all the way and kill me like he's promised so often to do. Instead, he gives me an unpleasant smile.

"Your strength of spirit is admirable," he says. "I almost regret how quickly I will break it. Let's hope you apply this much vigour to your duties."

Silence falls between us and I let it stay. There's nothing to gain speaking with him. A wall made of pure Rurium steel will yield quicker than Theron Visclaud.

Asking him to see me as something above the dirt beneath his shoe is never going to work. Yet, it won't stop me from trying.

Not until I find my way out of here, at least.

The sign above the pair of black doors at the corridor's end proclaims it's the living area for slaves.

Well, that answers my earlier question.

Theron pauses before the doors, and I wait beside him. I'm both curious and reluctant to see what's inside. Then, as if he's reconsidered, he turns away abruptly and takes a left into a shorter corridor.

I follow him hurriedly into a lift which he directs to the main floor.

The lift announces our arrival, and the doors open into the bustle of workers of the Andrak.

Polished glass and gleaming chrome surrounds us, the ceiling high and arched. The Andrak is the residence of the Konai, and all important members that serve as the government of Andrasar.

Everything seems so modern and advanced compared to the quaint village in Yoah I've lived in for twenty-two *enur*.

Most of the people I see milling about are Andrasari dressed in unwrinkled clothing, wearing polished shoes, and possessing the appearance of a life of care and comfort.

The rest are humans covered in unflattering grey, metal collars around the necks. Some wear a simple dress with sleeves that reach the elbows, the hemming down to the calves, and a tie around the waist to keep the ends of the dress from falling open. The others wear coveralls with no pockets.

The humans here don't look as beaten and abused as what I've seen outside of the Andrak. Ostensibly, being in direct servitude to the Konai has its benefits.

The stares of some Andrasari follow me as I walk behind Theron. Self-consciousness and embarrassment weighs on my shoulders because of my appearance. The forest wasn't kind to my clothing, and I know I look dirty and ratty.

Dragon's Captive

Facing straight ahead, I tell myself the Andrasari regarding me with distaste don't matter to me. I don't know these people and I don't care what they think of me. Since many of them believe all humans are filthy and disgusting, then I guess my raggedy appearance will solidify that belief.

Finally, Theron leads me into an infirmary. Its white walls and stark lighting is almost blinding, and there's an anti-septic odour. At the large desk stationed near the entrance are two Andrasari beings dressed in white coats.

They both greet Theron, but it's only the female who meets my gaze as the male picks up his tablet and hurries away.

The Andrasari female's dark hair is pulled back into a tie, though a good portion of her hair hides the left side of her face. She is beautiful, her features familiar for some reason. When I glance at her name stitched into her coat, I know why.

Eyin Visclaud. Theron's sister and *Nai sa* of Andrasar.

"Hello," she says, smiling. She greets me in the way Andrasari greet their peers by pressing her hand to her chest and dipping her head.

"Hello," I say, surprised. Awkwardly, I greet her the same way. I don't need to look at Theron to know he disapproves. His disdain exudes from him in waves.

"I hear you're my *rah*'s saviour," she says, coming around the desk. Then she does something even more surprising than greeting me as a friend. She clasps my hands in hers. Her golden eyes are filled with genuine emotion and gratitude. "Thank you."

My eyes wide, I nod silently. I'd never wanted or expected any gratitude for what I'd done. But Theron's loved ones would be happy he's still standing and capable of his usual terror.

Her gaze flickers to my neck and her lips tighten. She shifts a glare to Theron.

"Why did you collar her?"

"She is a human," says Theron as if that alone explains it. "As I've told you before, she is a flight risk."

"Then let her go," she says. This is Theron's sister? That's hard to believe. I was always certain the only members of the Visclaud family who didn't hate humans were dead. Maybe I was wrong.

"Stop undermining me, Eyin," he says, irritated. "Get on with your work. There are other things I need to do instead of chaperoning a human."

Eyin scowls, ready to retort when I speak up.

"Why was I brought to the infirmary?"

Her scowl softens when she looks at me.

"I'd like to give you a scan," she says. "Theron told me you fell when you helped remove the blades. I want to make sure nothing is broken."

"I'm fine. I don't hurt anymore."

"No harm in making sure."

Although she is genuinely friendly, I don't feel comfortable. Especially with Theron's presence like a dark cloud robbing the room of light.

Eyin regards me like someone who's found a lost, injured baby animal. I feel as much. No-one I love is alive. I'm alone in an incredibly unfamiliar and hostile territory, among strangers who hate me because I exist.

"All right," I say, relenting. It's not as if I've a real choice. Theron would simply zap me again and drag me off to be examined.

Eyin guides me to a room with a wide, rectangular metal table planted in its center. She instructs me to lie on its surface and, silently, I do as she asks. The table's surface lights up blue and Eyin retrieves a tablet, a frown of concentration on her forehead as she peers at the screen.

Tired of looking at the ceiling, my head lolls to the side and my gaze connects with Theron's.

He doesn't look away and neither do I. That warmth I felt last night in the pit of my stomach manifests again. He's tall and built so solidly. It must be hard not to notice him even in a crowded room. Literally impossible not to notice him now as his gaze holds mine.

In the same instance I wonder if his wounds have fully healed, I remind myself I shouldn't give a damn. This bastard imprisoned me, abducted me, zapped me and enslaved me. Not necessarily in that order, but these truths ought to be at the forefront of my brain whenever I look at him. The moronic attraction really ought to go fling itself in the path of a *draki*'s fire breath.

So, I finally look away from him. After scanning me, Eyin has me sit up. She shifts a curious gaze between me and Theron before she retrieves a syringe and approaches me with it.

"Inoculation," she says at my suspicious gaze. "You and I don't have the miraculous blood of the Shifted to fight off diseases."

Knowing she's an *Unshifted*—a Rur being incapable of achieving a dragon form—makes her less threatening. That isn't to say Unshifted Rur beings are any less dangerous than their Shifted counterparts. They are still faster and stronger than humans. Eyin might be amiable, but I don't doubt she can kill me in the blink of an eye if, for any reason, she sees me as a threat.

She leans forward to administer the shot in my arm. The hair on the side of her face shifts, revealing a long, jagged, bumpy scar across her cheek beneath her left eye.

Who could have done that to her?

After administering the shot, she nervously adjusts her hair so it covers her face again.

"You shouldn't hide it," I say to her. It's probably rude to comment on her scar, but she has been the only friendly face I've seen in a long time. There's an impulse in me to show her some sort of kindness in return. "Scars tell an interesting story."

"The story of this scar isn't interesting at all," she says as she helps me down from the table. "It's a boring tale of a little girl who hadn't learned yet how to keep her mouth shut."

"And it's one that the human needn't know because it's none of her business," says Theron, drawing closer. "Are you finished here?"

"Yes," Eyin says, throwing a quick frown at Theron before smiling at me. "Nothing broken. Some bruising, but rest will cure that and no strenuous activity will cure that."

Smiling at her in return, I feel a bit less hopeless about my situation. It's still terrible, but knowing that the Nai sa of Andrasar seems to be on my side gives me hope that maybe I can find my way out of Theron's clutches.

Theron and I leave the infirmary and make our way into one of the lifts again. But instead of taking us down, he touches the button for the highest floor.

"I thought you were taking me to the living area for slaves," I say.

"Is that where you'd like to be?" he asks, surprising me with a response.

"You know exactly where I want to be," I say, scowling at him. "Even your own *rahsa* thinks I should be—"

"Be quiet," he says coldly. "Ever since I met you you've been nothing but a thorn in my side."

Silence falls between us as the lift climbs. It feels strange for a *draki* like Theron to need these machines. In dragon form they're not inhibited by gravity.

"Sensible people don't keep things or people around them that annoy them," I say, unwilling to obey his order. It's apparent I have a death wish.

"You're right. They destroy them."

"Is that another allusion to killing me? Why don't you just go ahead and do it?"

"Because as much as you try to pretend you don't fear death or me, I know you fear us both, human. You have a stubborn spirit. One filled with so much hope that if you push harder and survive longer, things will get better for you. Salvation will come." His smile is as cold as his voice. "But it won't. It never does."

Amid the chiding tone, there's a bitterness in his voice that says he speaks from personal experience. What happened to him to make him hold onto such a depressing outlook on life?

"What's the point of living without some hope for better things?" I ask, but he returns to his typical behaviour and responds with chilly silence.

The lift stops, the doors sliding open to admit us onto a balcony. Spread out below is the stunning view of Andrasar City. I pause to admire the varying heights of the buildings, and the greenery interspersed amid the glassy buildings.

However, Theron's voice intrudes on my appreciation.

"Stop dragging your feet and let's go."

"This is my first time seeing the city."

"Today is a day of firsts for you."

"More bad than good ones," I mutter.

He ignores me and leads me to a door he unlocks with his palm against a translucent circle. We enter a room dominated by masculine colours. There's not much personality here, except for the modern and expensive furniture, but there's no denying that this place houses someone wealthy and important.

"Is this where you live?"

"Yes."

He opens another door that's on the right hand wall leading toward the entrance. He indicates I go ahead of him. I hesitate, but my curiosity and his glower carries me forward.

It's tiny in here, the trappings almost as sparse as my prison cell. At least the narrow bed looks sort of comfortable.

"And this," speaks Theron before I can say anything, "is where you'll be staying while you serve me as my *zevyet*."

Chapter Seven

Theron

The human does not fight me as I'd expected.

She makes no comment on the matter. She simply regards me with dislike. Despite it all, I still find her beautiful.

"Bathe and get rid of those rags you are wearing," I order her in harsh tones, irritated by the treacherous thoughts in my head. I indicate the door that leads to the bath, then the folded clothing I had another slave brought up for her. "Put those on and meet me outside."

Unwilling to be near her with a bed conveniently beside us luring me to make a horrible mistake, I leave without waiting for her response.

Seated at the table in the main room, I try to focus on the female close by who is naked in the bath. *She is a human*, I remind myself. No matter how hard my dragon insists that she is mine to take and enjoy, I will not go against my beliefs.

I let work swallow me into its depths. As long as time exists, so does work. As the Overseer, there are always decisions to make, proposals to read and approve, disputes to settle, missives to send. Many of my duties should be Aphat's, but he foists it all on me while he lazes away his days, enjoying the fruits of being a Konai.

But it's not a complaint that I have so much to do. I enjoy it. What I do furthers the advancement of Andrasar. When my father was the Konai, he would tell me his dreams of what he wanted to see this great region become.

I didn't understand it much at the time. As a child, I only marvelled that my father was the greatest being in all of Andrasar. Now I do. He had so much love for this region. My mother would joke that Andrasar was my father's second mate.

I frown at the time that has elapsed since I left the human to bathe. How long do these beings take to clean themselves?

She's concocting some means of escape.

Some humans are as intelligent as they are conniving. I'm about to investigate what she's doing when she exits the room.

She hesitantly approaches me where I sit. She's even more beautiful now that she has scrubbed away the dirt from her skin. The tatters she wore are replaced with the slave robes I gave her.

Her wild curls have been tamed into a long braid. I am amazed she managed to wrestle her wild curls into submission. I preferred when her hair was loose. Those curls were meant to be free, to be coiled around my fingers while I bent her over my desk and made her scream my name.

"What took you so long?" I ask her irritably. "I dislike waiting longer than is necessary, human."

She doesn't look the least bit repentant. This is the thing that I admire in her and but also infuriates me. She is wilfully disobedient despite knowing how easily I can destroy her if I wish.

"Is anger your only emotional setting?" she asks. "That must get tiring."

"What's tiring is having a disrespectful slave."

"I am not a slave."

"You are mine, now."

She opens her mouth and then snaps it shut, glaring at me. Clearly she had something even more disrespectful to say and decided not to speak it.

Smart girl.

She closes her eyes briefly and takes a deep breath as if she's summoning from some hidden source of inner strength.

"I'm sorry I took so long. I'm not intentionally disobeying you," she says. "These are new surroundings to me. Please be patient with me while I familiarize myself."

She seems sincere and it disturbs me. I dislike this feeling I have regarding her. Humans have always been invisible to me, like furniture. They exist for whatever purpose they were meant for. Nothing more.

This human... *Seela* is different.

I exist. You can see me and hear me.

It's as if my surroundings have only ever existed in black and white, but here she is, this vibrant spot of colour that captivates me.

"We will be visiting a mining plant in the Vak province tomorrow. There have been reports of rebellions brewing among the workers."

All that calm and sincerity she portrayed disappears. She looks at me with distrust.

"Are you going to kill them?"

"They deserve no less for their insubordination, but I will not kill them unless they've forced my hand," I say. "I will have you, a human, speak to them. Tell them how much more sensible it is to remember their place."

"As slaves?" she asks bitterly.

"What else?"

"That would only strengthen their need to rebel. After all, they're already reminded everyday of what they are to you."

"Clearly they've forgotten if they think they have the power to rise up against their *zevyena*."

She shakes her head. "They're not rebelling because they believe they have the power to challenge you. They're rebelling because they have no power at all except the *will* to fight."

"Will does not equal ability. Will alone does not win a fight."

"Sometimes, it can," she says with a shrug. "If you can take several damaging blows from your opponent but have the resilience to outlast him, who's the victor then?"

"Are you a rebel supporter, human?"

"If I were, I wouldn't be foolish enough to tell you," she says. "I don't support fighting, whether it's humans against Andrasari or Andrasari against humans. Our differences can be resolved without bloodshed."

"Yet you stabbed me twice in the arm."

"In self-defense after you threatened to kill me and chased after me when I attempted to flee."

At least she has the grace to look repentant, but no apology leaves her lips. Admittedly, I don't want it either.

Intrigued by a view into her mind, I am inclined to continue the conversation. However, there are other matters I must attend to.

I hand her the tablet with the speech I want her to read at the mining plant tomorrow. Her forehead creases in a frown as she peers at the screen.

"Can you read?"

She looks up from the tablet sharply. "Being a human isn't synonymous with being illiterate."

"It isn't because you are human why I asked." I am amused by her offended look. "You are from Yoah, home of the determinedly uneducated."

"Ikkon took my education seriously and weighed me down with any books he could find." There's a wistful look on her face. She drops her gaze to the tablet's screen again before darting a look at me. "Maybe it would be best if the speech were in Human Standard and not in Rur language?"

"Then rewrite it," I say, surprising the both of us.

"Thank you," she says quietly as I stand in preparation to leave. "Thank you for trying to avoid unnecessary loss of lives."

I'm gripped by her stare. In the infirmary I realized her eyes are not black as I'd assumed last night, but umber like the earth after a heavy rainfall. Her lips, plump and dusky pink, are unsmiling. They're no less tempting than when she asked me earlier what I'd reward her for good behaviour.

"Do not mistake my practical decision for some sort of *change* toward freedom for humans. That's never going to happen. The mining plant in Vak produces significant amounts of processed Rurium steel, and thus, profit to Andrasar. Killing swathes of the humans will necessitate a tedious process of hiring new workers. The new workers will harbour resentment about the fate of those before them, and the cycle would only repeat itself."

She frowns. "I understand."

I make my way toward the door, then turn and glare at her. "Don't try to escape while I'm gone. You will not succeed and I will punish you for attempting it."

Her forehead creases in a scowl. She mutters an insult I hear perfectly and which I should turn around and discipline her for, but I continue on my way out the door and down to Ronan's office.

When I enter his office, I find him facing one of the large windows overlooking the courtyard. Ronan is a sturdily built male of moderate height with hair lightened to silver.

His shoulders are often squared as if any minute he might need to fight an opponent. I suppose for someone who has dedicated his whole life to enforcing the law in Andrasar, he doesn't know how to shut off his need for constant vigilance.

"Theron, Eyin told me about the attack," Ronan greets when he sees me. "Good to see you alive and well."

I join him where he stands at the window. "I didn't tell Eyin the full story because I did not want to alarm her. I was led into a trap by a *zevyet* of the Andrak claiming you wanted to speak with me in a private location."

"That hardly sounds like something I would do," says Ronan, coolly. "I would have spoken with you via implant."

"In hindsight, it was foolish to believe the human, but he hurried away so quickly I felt compelled to follow his directions."

Ronan's golden eyes shine with disapproval.

"Never trust humans, Theron. Those worthless cretins lie at every turn." His lips are a hard, angry line, his eyes burning with rage. "None of them deserve the air we let them breathe."

"The reason I came to tell you is that the humans attacked me with Rurium blades, an uncommon weapon for humans to possess," I say before he can launch into his usual long-winded spiel of his hatred of humans. "I want you to open an investigation, starting with those within the Andrak. There may be a traitor among us and I intend to find out who."

Chapter Eight

Theron

I've lived always lived by myself, content with the solitude.

The only interruption on my quiet I welcome is Eyin coming to tell me about her day or a new discovery she made in her work. Whatever females I've had in my home often leave soon after we've had use of each other.

But Seela is here to stay. Well, as long as she serves her purpose. I'd prefer her being out of sight and therefore out of mind, but she putters around my quarters, lifting this, poking that, making unnecessary noises that distract me from my work.

Granted, I've an office I can use and sequester myself from Seela and her noise. I tell myself I don't

Dragon's Captive

use it because I want to keep an eye on her, and make sure she doesn't do anything foolish like try to run away.

I know the truth of the matter is that I enjoy watching her.

Like now as I sit at the table pretending to work. Instead, I watch her prepare my morning meal. There's no wall dividing the kitchen from the main room, so my view of her is uninterrupted.

Today is her second day as my slave and it is obvious many of the appliances are unfamiliar to her. She's truly a yokel if she's from the rural, backwater province of Yoah.

I know she knows I'm watching her. Her movements are too mechanical. More than once I've caught her glancing at me before quickly looking away. Each time she does this, her shoulders hunch and her body tightens as if it's to protect herself.

As if she's afraid of me.

She should be.

When she's finished preparing the meal, she brings the tray over and sets the dish down before me. What she's prepared looks palatable and has a delicious scent, but I don't eat it right away.

The meals I had before Seela's arrival and up to last night were prepared by Andrasari cooks. I've never dared eat from the hands of a human.

"You don't like it?" she asks.

"I haven't tasted it yet to judge."

"You think I poisoned it, don't you?"

"Is it?"

"Of course it isn't!" she snaps. She bites her lips together beneath my look of consternation. Breathing slowly, she softens her voice. "You were watching me the entire time."

"Humans are stealthy when they have evil intentions."

"Anyone can be stealthy when they're up to no good." She shakes her head. "What's the point of having me as your *zevyet*? You don't trust me and I don't want to be here."

It's a question I've asked myself several times already but I haven't found an answer that I can accept. I've told myself she might be useful in my fight against the rebellions, but there are many other humans who can do the job without being in such close proximity to me.

The real answer: she is my *asafura*, and whether I like it or want to accept it, I can't let her go.

"You are useful, that's why you're here." I indicate the tablet. "I've noticed you've made changes to the speech. While most of it is passable, I got rid of the other unnecessary additions."

She purses her lips. "I didn't know you could read Human Standard."

"I would be foolish not to learn the language of my enemy if I need to defeat them."

"The history books will laud your efficient tyranny, *zevyena*," she says, her tone laced with sarcasm.

I scowl. "Use that tone with me again and I will remind you of the purpose of that collar around your neck and how tyrannical I can be."

She glares. "Is there anything else you require of me?"

"Eat something," I tell her as I begin chewing on what she prepared for me. To my surprise, it's very good. "We leave soon and the journey to Vak is some distance."

She gives me a strange look but says nothing as she returns to the kitchen and busies herself there.

Soon, we leave and make our way to the Andrak's air cruiser port. Air cruisers are a weak imitation of flight travel, often only used by the Unshifted or elderly Andrasari who cannot maintain their dragon form for long.

But I cannot shift into my dragon for the journey as I'm taking Seela with me. When we climb into the air cruiser, all of her chilliness from our earlier conversation dissipates, replaced by interest and excitement.

Her fingers dig into the sides of her seat as we take off and only relax after she's grown accustomed to the speed. She peers out through the transparent glass hood of the cruiser at Andrasar City below us.

"It's because of mining why humans are here on Rur," she says suddenly. "Excessive mining for the sake of advancement. It led to a radiation leak that killed millions before my ancestors managed escape."

I sense a lesson of some sort in her preachy tones. "What's the purpose of this story?"

She turns away from the view zooming by outside to award me a tight smile.

"Andrasar should hope that history doesn't repeat itself. That their quest for rapid advancement doesn't lead to the destruction of their lands and Rur as a whole. That they're not forced to relocate to another planet where its inhabitants might mistreat them."

"You can rest easy knowing that history will not repeat itself. Rur beings are far stronger than humans can ever hope to be."

Nevertheless, her words discomfort me because within them there is some truth.

The Rur way has always been to never take more than what Kahafura has given us. We don't ravage our lands. But when Aphat became the Konai, all he sought was riches and he found it in the thick Rurium veins inhabiting Andrasar.

The precious metal is mined in large quantities and sold to neighbouring regions. Some of our beautiful forests have already been destroyed, the land gouged out. There have been reports that the waters near some mining sites are being poisoned by the dangerous chemical leaks due to unsafe mining procedures.

Implementing safer mining procedures have been an uphill battle due to some of the mining companies' resistance to change. However, threats of large financial penalties and lengthy imprisonment often work to ensure their compliance.

We journey the rest of the way in silence. When we arrive at the mining site, it is alive with activity. The mid-morning sun awards us with pleasant warmth, an acrid scent in the air from the mines.

The mining site's area manager approach us as soon as we get out of the cruiser. He casts a disdainful glance at Seela that irks me before he regards me with a simpering smile and a flamboyant showing of respect.

"Nai Theron, it is an honour to have you in our presence this fine morning," he says. "I will have the humans gather right away to hear your speech."

"I won't be the one speaking today," I say. "My *zevyet* will be the voice. It is my hope they will listen to reason from their own kind."

He nods emphatically. "A wise decision. And if all else fails, then we will have no choice but to kill them all."

Seela stiffens at this. She's about to open her mouth and cause trouble for herself, so I order the area manager to lead us to where she'll read her speech.

We are surrounded by nothing but red dirt, the ground uneven as we walk. When Seela loses her balance, I reach for her immediately, catching her by the waist. Her soft body feels good against me. Too good. I hold onto her a few seconds longer than necessary. She gazes up at me as she mutters a soft thanks, her dark brown eyes a leash on my soul.

The temptation to drag her to the red, dusty floor and kiss her until she slaps my chest for air is so strong, I pull her a little closer in preparation to do it.

"Watch your step so you don't fall flat on your face," I tell her harshly when I remember myself and where we are. I release her. I always do this when she affects me. I push her away with my words in the hopes of pushing away the feelings and thoughts she inspires in me. "I won't help you again."

"Yes, *zevyena*," she says coldly, looking away from me.

A makeshift podium is erected as the area manager sounds the order for the humans to gather near it. The humans accumulate before us, their skin and clothing covered in red dust. Their expressions range from open hostility to apathy, and I already suspect a speech isn't going to change their minds away from defiance.

Beside me, Seela visibly struggles to subdue her fear. It's strange that an individual who faced down a dragon several times her size now trembles before a crowd of her own people.

"Convince them or they will have to perish," I remind her as I hand her the tablet. She nods silently and takes the tablet with trembling hands.

Squaring her shoulders, Seela begins to read the speech. Her voice is clear and smooth, conveying the message of Andrasar's might and the consequences to those who challenge it with foolish notions of rebellions.

Midway through, a lone voice shouts out a word in Human Standard.

"Traitor!"

Seela stumbles over her words and darts a worried at me but forges ahead. More voices begin to shout *traitor* at her. She cuts off her speech.

"I am not a traitor," she says angrily. The area manager looks to me as if awaiting my order to punish the humans, but I shake my head. I want to see how this proceeds first before we intervene. "I'm trying to prevent a needless war."

"They've taken everything we have already!" shouts a human near the front of the crowd, his neck bulging with fury. "Fighting's all we got left!"

"You still have your lives," Seela says. "There are other ways to effect change other than through killing."

The crowd has become restless. More voices shouting as the humans get angrier by the second. A thick piece of metal comes sailing out from the midst of the crowd directly at Seela.

I pull her out of harm's way, shielding her so the metal strikes me instead. A cacophony of angry shouts erupts as the area manager orders the Andrasari guards to subdue the crowd.

Rage rises within me, my dragon bristling with fury. Not because of the pain from where the metal has struck me, but because these humans had intended to harm Seela.

A riot erupts and I release Seela. My clothing tears away from me as my body morphs into my dragon form. I will kill them. I will burn them all. I was foolish to think that they would listen to anything else but fire searing them alive.

I roar, the fire burning in my belly. Everyone, even the other Andrasari, grow frozen and silent.

Then a voice cries my name plaintively.

"Please don't kill them, Theron," Seela begs. "Please."

Everything within me says I should ignore her plea to spare the humans' lives. They deserve no less than death by fire. But there's a look in her eyes that says if I do it, if I kill them, she will never forgive me for it.

I shouldn't care whether I have her forgiveness or not. I shouldn't care what she thinks of me. I am her master and she is my slave. I am a monster and she is a naive, innocent creature that has somehow wandered into my clutches.

But it's that look in her eyes. That look that made me spare her life after she saved mine. Like she's given up hope. In what? I don't know. Yet I don't like it. As much as I accept that I am a monster, I don't like that I am the one that makes her feel this way.

So I retreat to my primary form. Clamping a hand on her arm, I guide her wordlessly back to the air cruiser.

Chapter Nine

Seela

Twenty-six *detar* has passed since I became a dragon's captive.

The time has gone by so quickly, I can't believe it's been that long. Furthermore, I can't believe that in that space of time, I've not found my escape.

Though, if I'm being honest, I have not sought it like I'd planned. Like I'm supposed to. In moments like these when I'm by myself, shrouded by the darkness in my room, I'm forced to listen to the words of those humans from the mining plant in my head over and over again.

Traitor. Traitor.

I had a chance to end this. Or at least, make the fight for humans a lot easier to achieve our freedom.

I didn't. Not for the first time, I second guess my actions. Had I let Theron die, I would be free right this moment and not be captive as his slave.

Several chances to take his life are afforded me, but I don't do it. I don't even want to attempt it.

Instead, I continue in my treacherous behaviour by being attracted to him. By remembering the feel of his hands around me when he saved me from the attack at the mining plant. By letting stupid hope foster that I can get through to him because he listened to me when I begged him not to kill the humans.

He didn't do it because you asked, he did it because it was more trouble than it was worth.

In the time I've known Theron, I've learned that he is not one to make purposeless decisions or actions. He was raised to hate humans. He didn't spare their lives because he'd suddenly developed a conscience.

I slide off my bed and stand.

"Lights on," I say. The diminutive room floods with light.

As I put on clean clothing, I wonder if this is why I haven't escaped. Am I an animal? Did I trade my freedom for a collar because it meant a roof over my head, a soft bed, and food in my belly?

If I were still free, I'd still be living in the forest, still always on the brink of starvation or dehydration, fighting against not only nature, but fear of discovery from other Andrasari dragons who might not have been as accommodating with my life as Theron.

Traitor!

The voice is louder than ever, but I drown it out as I prepare myself for another day as my enemy's servant.

Even though it's already morning, it's still dark. I like to get up early as it was a habit I acquired when I worked with Ikkon in the bakery. We'd rise before the sun and get as much baking done so everything was fresh for our customers.

There was often so much work to do in the bakery. Here in the Andrak, I have more time on my hands than I need as Theron's slave. I am nothing but a housekeeper trapped in an already spotless home.

The most I do is prepare his meals which he eats with nary a sound of appreciation. Not that it annoys me or that I'm looking for it. If I were to hold my breath in expectation of gratitude from Theron, I'd die from lack of oxygen.

Sometimes he gives me miscellaneous tasks related to his work, but never anything that contains important information.

Dragon's Captive

Yet another area where I fail my people, I guess. As a slave to Andrasar's Overseer, I am in the perfect position to glean as much information that can possibly aid in the rebellion. Another thing I don't do.

I can't, either, because Theron makes sure to keep the doors to his bedroom and office locked.

He has an impressive library and a console. To my surprise, he lets me use both, so I spend a good portion of my time reading or watching a show.

He has a sizable collection of rare and old books. Even books that were in the possession of the first generation of humans to set foot on Rur.

Sometimes, I don't feel like a prisoner here. Sometimes, I even forget that there's a metal ring around my throat marking me as property to another being.

Inevitably, Theron reminds me all over again. As if it's also to remind himself.

I have just finished preparing his morning meal when I hear the sound of his footsteps approaching.

My awareness of him immediately strengthens. I'm in this strange place where Theron is concerned. Half of me resents him for who he is and what he's done, while the other half of me notices the breadth of his shoulders in his jacket, the deepness of his voice when he speaks, his clean scent whenever I'm near him.

There's this thing between us. Something heavy that thickens the air when we're in each other's presence. I often convince myself I'm being paranoid.

But then there are the moments when I accidentally touch him as I hand him something and a delicious little shiver curls along my spine from the touch. Or the way his amber eyes darken to burnt gold when he looks at me sometimes.

Over and over I have to convince myself I'm misreading things. That every so often he doesn't look at me like if he wants to consume me.

After all, what do I know about these things when I've only ever had one hasty encounter with a male? Besides, I have as much value to him as the utensils I set down beside his plate. I am nothing more than a tool for him to use and then discard when I can no longer function.

He's seated at the table where he likes to sit and follow my every moment. Probably because he's still suspicious I will add poison to his meals. I set down what I've prepared for him and retreat to the kitchen to tidy up the area.

When I'm done, so is he with his meal. As I retrieve the used dishes, I decide to try my luck.

Dragon's Captive

"Can I go to Yoah?" I ask, mustering a sincere and respectful tone.

"No," he says right away. He doesn't even lift his gaze from the screen of his tablet as he scribbles on it.

I frown. I hadn't anticipated a positive response, but he denied me with such crushing finality it irks me.

"You don't want to know why I want to go to Yoah?"

"I know it's a ploy for you to abandon your duties as my slave."

"It isn't," I say, though I won't lie it hasn't crossed my mind. "I want to see what became of my home."

"Then perhaps you should have turned back when you were in the forest," he looks at me then, a glower on his features.

Then I would be dead and wouldn't have to endure you being your usual bastard self.

The words don't leave my mouth but he glares at me as though he's heard them nonetheless. Maybe my expression shows how much I dislike him right now. He is excellent at hiding his emotions, but I literally wear my heart outside my body.

"Even if I were foolish enough to entertain your request, now is not a good time," he says as he stands.

"I am leaving for a conference in Seca today."

"When will you return?" And why do I feel disappointed at the news that he is leaving?

"In seven *detar*."

Seven days by myself in this prison?

I frown. "And I'll continue to be chained here with nothing to do."

"I can make your exaggerations come through and chain you indeed." He glares at me. "You will serve the Andrak while I'm gone and you will stay among the other slaves until I return."

"Why can't I come with you?" I can't believe I've voiced those words. I want to pull them back into me as soon as they're out there. Theron gives me a strange look as he regards me silently.

"Perhaps another time," he says, surprising me.

He touches his implant and orders someone to send up another slave.

Shortly after his call while I'm watering his plant—its presence in Theron's home continues to stupefy me since I wouldn't have expected him of all people to nurture anything—a soft knock sounds on the door.

Theron voices a command to his security system and the door unlocks. A human female with pale skin and wavy, dark hair to her shoulders enters the room.

Dragon's Captive

She greets Theron respectfully and gives me a tiny wave, a small smile on her light pink lips. Dressed in a loose-fitting coverall, she is slim with a lovely, oval-shaped face and hooded, close-set eyes.

"She will be your guide while I'm gone," says Theron. "Go with her now."

It's so sudden. I wonder if I should go to my room and retrieve anything I might need. I don't bother as the other human turns and heads for the door. I follow her closely, too excited at the prospect of finally being free of Theron's home and possibly making my escape from the Andrak.

But just before I can step through the door, Theron grasps my wrist and forces me to look at him. His golden eyes burn into me and sees my intentions.

"Don't be foolish," he says, his voice low and filled with a warning. "Even when I'm gone, you will continue to obey me, Seela. Take one step beyond the gates of the Andrak and I will know."

Chapter Ten

Seela

The human female and I make our introductions as we head to the lift.

Her name is Xia and she works with her father helping to keep the lights on in the Andrak.

On the ride down the lift, I fume over Theron's words. Even if he'll know I've left the Andrak, he'll be far from Andrasar and unable to stop me.

Or find me for that matter.

Just because I've been his obedient slave for almost a month doesn't mean I intend to be that forever. He might have called me foolish for considering to make my escape, but he's the foolish one for thinking his threats will stop me from trying.

Dragon's Captive

"Even if you do escape, how will you get the collar off without his authorization?" asks Xia.

Does everyone here possess the ability to read minds?

"How did you know—"

"It's written all over your face," she says, smiling. "Lesson One of being a *zevyet* of the Andrak: learn to hide what you're thinking. Lesson Two: if you're plotting an escape, make sure you don't half-ass it or you'll regret it."

"You sound like you're speaking from experience."

"I was born and grew up here," Xia says. "I've witnessed others attempt escape, fail and suffer the consequence for it."

Xia and I arrive at our destination and we get off. Her words have instilled doubt. She didn't discourage me. She told me what I needed to hear. I need a solid plan if I want to escape.

"Have you ever wanted to leave?" I ask her.

"Where would I go? Everyone I know is here," she says, but her voice lacks conviction. Of course it's a lie. Every being likes freedom. "How did you become Nai Theron's *zevyet*? You're new. Only those who've served within the Andrak for several years and have shown loyalty to their service end up becoming a slave to someone of such a high position."

"I did him a favour and this is how he thinks it fit to repay me," I say bitterly. I don't want to tell her the truth. I'm afraid if I do I'll make an enemy of her and all the other humans here in the Andrak.

Xia leads me to the slaves' living area. It's militaristic in design with bland, grey walls just like the corridors we came through. There are rows of bunk beds, all of them properly made. Small metal bedside tables are covered with personal effects that somewhat lightens the gloominess of the room.

"Probably not as nice as what you have in your *zevyena*'s home," says Xia.

"His home is my prison."

Xia gives me a curious look. "Were you free when he found you?"

I hesitate to answer, but I decide on the truth.

"Yes."

"Usually, he locks up humans he's found without a collar. You must have done him a pretty big favour."

I smile tightly but don't respond. Instead, I wander about the room, and decide to change the subject.

"So, what's our mission today?"

"Well, the Andrak has just underwent expansion and getting the new sections wired has been a real pain in the ass," Xia says. "We could use your help for the simpler tasks."

"Sounds fun. I like learning new things."

Xia grins. "Talk to me after you've tripped a few times over a bunch of wires. Or zapped yourself by accident."

"You said 'simpler' tasks. I won't be touching anything likely to fry me. If I wanted to get a zapping, I'll just anger my master."

"That shouldn't be funny but it is," Xia says, chuckling. "So, one more thing: curfew's at nine. You have to be back here before that or the doors will be locked. You'll either have to hide somewhere until the morning or they'll punish you. Come with me and I'll show you around."

Xia takes me on a brief tour of the important areas of the Andrak. With so many buildings, the Andrak is like its own small village in the heart of Andrasar City.

Even though Xia has done her best to show me the routes to the places I might need to go, I'm already certain I'll get lost. At least there are maps appended to the walls. Hopefully I won't get too lost if I use those.

Finally, she leads me to the new building where she works. Wires are strewn everywhere. Six other humans are in various locations of the spacious, empty room. The noisiness from their tools are so jarring, I wince.

"You'll get used to it," shouts Xia.

The others chuckle and greet me warmly and I do the same. It's strange being among so many other humans. All my life the only company I've had was Ikkon in the bakery.

Most Andrasari customers didn't want to interact with a human. I'd hide away in the back while Ikkon dealt with them, much to his consternation.

He'd say he didn't care if he lost an Andrasari customer who didn't want a human attending to them, but I didn't like knowing someone didn't want to buy from us because of me.

During a lull in the noise, a slim male with thinning dark hair streaked silver comes over to greet us. Xia introduces him as her father, Shihong.

"I'll give you some early advice, Seela," he says with a friendly smile as he points at Xia. "Be careful of this one. I raised a monster. She'll bite your head off like a *draki* if she catches you slacking."

Xia rolls her eyes. "Dad, you were sleeping."

Shihong pouts. "There's no crime in a nap."

"No, but if you take one with a drill lying on your stomach, it's reason enough for you to get yelled at."

Dragon's Captive

"You worry too much," Shihong says, then he pats her cheek in a fatherly gesture of love. "Just like your mother, Kahafura bless her."

Their exchange makes me smile, but it leaves me wistful, reminding me of what I lost when Ikkon was taken from me.

With Xia's guidance, I'm set on the task of wire maintenance for the next few days. Unravelling them, feeding them into a machine to have them cut, sometimes passing Xia tools as she needs them.

Xia loves and takes pride in her work. She has a bossy edge she's not afraid to show in order to get the work done.

There is an easy and infectious camaraderie among the workers with Shihong at the head of it all. Every day, he regales us with jokes or stories about Earth.

"At one point there were a bunch of idiots who used to think that Earth was flat," he says as we pack things up in preparation to leave for dinner. It's my third day here, and I'm starting to like being among Xia, Shihong, and the rest of the crew. "Then, for a long time humans used to believe they were the only intelligent beings in existence."

"Just more proof that humans are stupid," says Xia, a bitterness in her voice. "The last of our kind and what do we do? We end up getting enslaved and killed off."

"It won't always be like this, Xia," he says quietly, his humour fading as his tone becomes somber. "Someday, humans will have their freedom again."

"You have to watch what you say, Shihong," says one of the workers with a grin. His name is Jogen, and I have a suspicion he and Xia are more than just friends. "If any of those *draki* bastards hear you they'll think you're one of those freedom fighters in the rebellion."

"Me? A fighter?" Shihong laughs. "I'm nothing but a coward. Besides, I have a daughter to take care of and I'm too old. Let the young ones fight the good fight."

"Maybe we can get our freedom back without any fighting," I speak up. "Not all Andrasari like how we're being treated."

I think of Ikkon who died because of me, of the other Andrasari beings who lost their lives in Yoah for not supporting our enslavement. I remember Eyin, the Nai sa, telling Theron to free me that first day.

Xia wears a look of extreme doubt, but Shihong nods.

Dragon's Captive

"All it would take is for a new Konai with a mind toward equality to come into power—"

He breaks off his sentence when the door slides open abruptly and a troop of Andrasari guards storm into the room. They cast a hard glance over all of us as they form a blockade before the door.

The way they're looking at us discomforts me. It's not just with the usual dislike. It's with a sinister sort of satisfaction and evil anticipation. As if they've caught us doing something we shouldn't and can't wait for us to pay for our wrongdoing.

A tall and stocky Andrasari male with greying hair pushes through to the front of the guards.

My heart thuds harder in my chest, my breath coming faster. There's no mistaking his features because I've seen it countless times in my nightmares.

Which means that if he's here, something is horribly wrong.

He smiles but I can't really call it that. It's his lips stretching over his teeth, baring them in an unsettling manner while his golden eyes swirl with hate. His golden eyes sweep over us with disgust. He doesn't make it known he recognizes me. As a human, I am forgettable to him.

He reaches into the pocket of his charcoal jacket and withdraws a plain-white rectangular card, holding it aloft. There is text written on it, but his fingers obscure it.

"Do you know what this is?" he asks. We're all tense and silent. "This is the key to the armory. Several days ago, the armory was breached and weapons were stolen." Then his awful gaze hones in on Xia whose face is stricken with terror. He steps right in front of her. "But you already knew this. I found the card in your possession."

Xia opens her mouth but no sound comes out. Shihong's features are tight with fear and anger. He forces himself between Xia and the Andrasari male.

"She doesn't, *Zevyena* Ronan," Shihong says, clenching his fists at his sides. "I found that card. I intended to return it—"

Shihong doesn't get to finish his response. The Andrasari named Ronan fists his hand and slams it into Shihong's stomach.

Crying out, Shihong staggers and bends over from the pain. Ronan doesn't relent. He knees him in the face before viciously swiping him with fingertips he's shifted into claws.

As one, we let out cries of anger. Xia and I reach for Shihong who is crumpled on the floor while the rest charge at Ronan and the guards.

The humans don't get very far. The Andrasari repel their attacks swiftly, killing a few of them while injuring the others. Shihong meant a lot to these people for them to sacrifice their lives to retaliate against the Andrasari.

"Your punishment for your thievery is death," Ronan spits at Shihong lying dazed on Xia's lap. Blood flows freely from Shihong's nose and where Ronan swiped him across the cheek. His left eye is puffy and rapidly turning purple. Ronan waves a hand over the rest of us. "Gather the others. They're to be imprisoned for insubordination."

"That's a lie!" I spit, my heart slamming in my chest. Outrage churns in me and robs me of logic that I keep my mouth shut. "We did nothing to you. You attacked first."

Ronan spins to face me, his eyes shining with perfect hatred. He raises his hand, intending to hit me when Xia shouts at him with tears in her eyes.

"She is Nai Theron's *zevyet*. If you hurt her, you'll be answering to him for abusing his property."

Ronan looks like he's still going to hit me and I don't flinch away. I'm rigid with rage and more than ready to kill him for the horrible things he's done. To Shihong, to Xia, to these humans, and to me.

He drops his hand to wrap steely fingers around my arm as he and his guards marches us to our imprisonment.

Chapter Eleven

Seela

They leave the dead behind. They throw the rest of us into one large cell.

Except Shihong.

As they carry him away, Xia begs them to take her instead with tears running freely from eyes. Ronan zaps her and for longer than necessary. She falls to the floor, her screams echoing off the glass walls as she shakes violently.

"Please, stop!" I beg him, swallowing my anger in fear for my friend's life. "Please! You'll kill her."

Ronan sneers at me, his intention clear that killing Xia is exactly what he wants to do. He lets up on Xia, storming off from the cells with his guards.

Dragon's Captive

Kneeling, I pull Xia into my lap. Her skin is hot and covered in sweat as she pants, her body twitching occasionally as she recovers from being zapped.

The rage returns, scalding in my chest. I feel Xia's pain as she cries because I have been here before. I have lost someone I loved without the power to stop it from happening.

"It's my fault," she whispers. "It's my fault he's going to die." She opens her eyes, pain swimming in their dark-brown depths. "I'm the one who found the armory key discarded on the floor. I didn't return it because I thought... I thought I could use it someday."

Smoothing a hand over her forehead, I muse on her words.

"But how did he know you had it?"

Fresh tears leak from her eyes as she sits up.

"What does it matter?" Xia says angrily. "They have my father now. He confessed to being the one who found the card, but they're charging him for thievery. There's never any justice for humans." She hangs her head and rests her face in her palms. "They're going to kill my father and it's all because I had some foolish hope we could be free. We'll never be free from this hell!"

"We'll get your father out, Xia," I say and reach to comfort her. She jerks away from my touch. I put more confidence in my words than I feel. "We'll figure something out."

Several hours pass, though I don't know how many. It's long enough to endure hunger pangs, long enough for tiredness to overcome us all.

We let Xia sleep on the one tiny bed available. The rest of us take the floor. It's heartbreaking to hear Xia's soft crying. I want to make things right for her but I feel helpless that I don't know how.

I could ask Theron for help, but the chance of him going against his peer's decision is low. Theron is loyal to his people and doesn't believe in fairness for humans.

Besides, he isn't in Andrasar and won't return for a few more days. By the time he's back, Shihong would have died and maybe the rest of us too.

"Shihong has always been like a father to me," says Jogen in anger. "He's served these bastards dutifully for years. If they kill him, that's it. I'm joining."

There's no need for me to ask him what he means by that. He's going to participate in the rebellions.

Eventually we're given a tiny meal. We try to feed it to Xia but she refuses to eat.

"You have to keep your strength up, Xia," I coax her.

"So that they can use it?" she spits. Her eyes are red from excessive crying. "Continue to use me after what they're going to do to my father?"

"Your father wouldn't want you to starve yourself."

"My father is dead."

"Not... he isn't dead." My voice is low and insistent. "Shihong cares for you and loves you, Xia. It'll hurt him to know you aren't taking care of yourself." I push the tray toward her. "Eat."

She shifts an angry gaze between me and the tray. I'm convinced she's going to deny the meal again. However she picks up the dry, shrivelled piece of meat and bites into it with a fierceness as if it's the thing causing her pain.

As she's finished eating, I hear footsteps approaching. We all stand, our tiredness abating as our fear is renewed. They're coming for us now. They're coming to end us all.

It's not at all what I expect.

It's Theron.

My lips part in amazement. Why is he here? A day at most has passed since we were imprisoned. He's supposed to be in Seca for at least a few more.

Snarling an order at the guards, he has the door to our cell unlocked and he steps inside. Everyone retreats at his entry, terror etched into their features. I almost do the same because Theron has a presence that captivates you and frightens you at the same time.

His gaze is fixed on me. He's angry. It burns in his golden eyes and radiates from him.

"I'm not gone long and yet you already defy me," he says in icy tones.

"I didn't," I say quickly, shaking my head. "Whatever you're told, it's all a lie."

"Be quiet," he orders. He casts a suspicious gaze around the others before he looks at me again. "Let's go."

I'm about to ask about the others, but he pivots and storms out of the cell. I look around at the other humans before I fix my gaze on Xia.

"I'll free your father," I promise her even though I know it's the worst thing to do. One shouldn't make promises they have no power to keep. Xia nods silently and I hurry out before Theron finds issue with me lagging behind.

He says nothing to me on our ride up the lift and I don't volunteer words either. When we're in the privacy of his home, I speak.

"I've seen the Andrasari named Ronan before." I rush to speak the rest of the words, determined to be heard before he shuts me down. "He's killed many Andrasari in my village who he deems supporters of the human rebellions."

"You're making some serious allegations." Theron scowls at me. "Why should I believe you when I've found you charged for attacking Ronan and his guards?"

So why did you free me from prison if you think I did it?

"I'm telling the truth," I say instead. "There were rumours going around Yoah that Andrasari who supported humans were being murdered. Then he showed up at the bakery. I saw him. I..." My voice breaks as I remember the horrible image of Ronan sinking his vicious claws into Ikkon's chest. "I watched him kill Ikkon right in front of me."

Theron is silent as he regards me, so I forge ahead. This might be my only chance I can get through to him.

"The humans who attacked only did so in retaliation." I recount the tale of what happened when Ronan stormed in. "I think..." I lick my lips slowly and lowers my voice. "I think it was a setup. I think he *wanted* Xia to find that card so he could accuse someone of wrongdoing. How could he have accurately discovered the card in her possession?"

Theron frowns and looks away from me as if in thought. Does he know something about this?

"Why didn't the human return the card the instant she found it?"

I hesitate. "Maybe she forgot to do it in time."

His stare bores into me, seeing the truth. Theron is as smart as he is ruthless. My heart sinks that he might want to punish Xia for something she'd planned but never did.

"How did you know I was imprisoned?" I ask, hoping to sidetrack him.

"News spreads quickly in the Andrak. Eyin heard and notified me."

Asking him if he cut his trip short for me would be nothing short of presumptuous, and likely to get me zapped for its insinuation that he cares about me.

"He's innocent," I say instead, referring to Shihong. "He doesn't deserve to die."

"No-one is innocent," he says. "Not even you. But you are naive to think anything can be done to save this human. He has confessed to having the card. That has sealed his fate."

"But you can help him, Theron." I move without thinking, reaching to touch his arm. He goes rigid.

Upset with myself I've overstepped and have lost my chance to help Shihong, I retract my hand hastily.

Theron grabs hold of my wrist and steps closer.

"I am and always will be your master. Therefore, you should refer to me as such and not by my given name as though we are equals."

"Yes, *zevyena*."

Scowling, I try to tug my hand away but his grip tightens.

"Did Ronan hurt you?"

His question comes out of nowhere, surprising me.

"Why do you care?" I ask bitterly. "I am human. My welfare means nothing to you."

"You mean something to me," he says. A fluttery sensation fills the pit of my stomach even though I try not to add any extra meaning to his words. "You belong to me. I don't take kindly to others damaging what's mine."

"Because you lose out on doing it yourself?"

"Do you remember what I told you, Seela? Never make me repeat a question."

It's unnerving having him so close, the heat of his fingers pressing directly against my skin.

"He didn't hurt me. He was going to until he learned I was yours... your *zevyet*." My face heats. "I guess he fears you more than he loves torturing humans."

We fall silent. His grip loosens on my arm but he still doesn't let me go. Instead he... he caresses me. His thumb moving along my skin slowly.

What would have happened to Ronan if he had hurt me? If I'd told Theron?

I want to ask him that question but my mind can't focus right now. Every bit of me is concentrated on that point of contact I share with him. It's such an innocent touch, but every tiny caress shoots an arrow of heat straight between my legs.

The pit of my stomach feels heavy and tight, like if something alive is in there. Our gazes are locked until his grow half-lidded as he focuses on my lips.

It's unmistakable this time. There's no denying the hunger darkening his gaze. I'm frozen with amazement by this and my heart thumps so loudly, I'm sure he hears it.

Traitor! I hear the human's voice from the mine in Vak so long ago. Goddess above, he's right. I've forgotten all about Shihong's demise, about Xia's pain, about the fact that Theron is my enemy. All I can think about is how much I want him to do what he clearly wants to do too.

Maybe just one kiss.

Just one kiss and then we can go back to perfect hatred of each other. He'll stay on his side of the wall and I'll stay on mine.

He leans closer, his lips hovering over mine. I wait for him to finish this, but it's as if he's waiting for me to stop him. When I don't, he drops my hand and lurches away from me.

His mask is gone and I see it all. The hunger and the hate. The conflict, the war that he's fighting inside himself. Then it's all shuttered away before I can blink.

"Go to your room, slave," he spits and I obey with haste.

I don't just run away from him, I hurry away with the hope that all that treacherous desire I'd felt for him would be left behind before it could catch up to me again.

Chapter Twelve

Theron

Perhaps I'm going insane.

Or at least some sort of sickness has taken over me. It can only explain why I let myself even consider kissing Seela let alone almost doing it.

What's worse is knowing that she waited for it. Her eyes begged me as much as her body did. The scent of her arousal goaded my dragon and I almost took the bait.

My cock is hard and I'm half convinced I should barge into her room after her and show her what she does to me.

I head outside instead. Climbing onto the balcony railing, I leap off and shift into my dragon mid-air. It's dangerous, but I enjoy the thrill of watching the ground rush toward me before I escape a gruesome impact with a few pumps of my wings.

The higher I fly, the cooler the atmosphere, and it calms me. Eventually, night arrives. It reminds me that I should have been at the conference in Seca, strengthening Andrasar's relationship with the region, one Aphat almost destroyed with a pointless war.

Instead I raced back to Andrasar when Eyin called me with the news of Ronan imprisoning the humans, Seela among them.

Why I would go to such lengths to ensure a human's safety is something I refuse to ponder. It's for the same reason why I don't want to read into the fury stewing inside me for Ronan. He dared to touch what is mine. He imprisoned her and threatened to harm her.

What Seela divulged about Ronan bothers me. How long has this been going and how have I not heard anything about it?

Trusting Seela seems unwise because it's hard for me to accept someone as good and honest like her exists. Yet I believe her. Even though I dislike humans because they constantly remind me of what I've lost, I've come to an apathetic acceptance of their presence in Andrasar.

However, the hate Ronan has for humans knows no comparison. I have aided in Aphat's campaign to terrorize them, but it thrives because of Ronan.

While I understand the reasoning behind it, I can't accept and support Ronan's injustices against our kind.

Returning home, I put on fresh clothing and resist the temptation to open Seela's door as I walk past it. I head to Ronan's office, finding him sharing company and a bottle of wine with Aphat.

Aphat levels his usual hostile stare at me, whereas I conceal the hatred I feel for him and greet him with respect.

"I didn't expect your return this early, Theron," says Ronan coolly, his gaze sharp. "Was the purpose of the conference unsuccessful?"

"The meetings were concluded sooner than anticipated," I say. "Seca accepted our peace offering and agreed to lift the trading ban against Andrasar."

"That old fuck dead yet?" Aphat asks, his eyes glittering with evil delight. "I heard he was set to meet Kahafura any moment."

"Nai Adan informed me his father is still alive."

A lie of course. Adan was tight-lipped about his *toha*'s health when I asked. Nevertheless, the words have the desired effect. Aphat's face goes sour like a child who's had his sweet stolen from his grasp.

Aphat started the war with Seca because of his greedy plans to claim dominion over the region. He sent countless Andrasari to their deaths to battle the ice dragons who had the advantage of imperviousness against unfavourably cold temperatures.

His hunger for power often unearths my old suspicions that he had a hand in my parents' deaths.

"I would like to have a word with Ronan in private, *Okan*," I say.

"I'm the fucking Konai," he spits, launching to his feet. Predictable as always in his dramatics. "I own Andrasar and everything within it. Even you, Theron. Whatever you have to say to Ronan can be said while I'm here."

Alcohol has given him the courage to challenge me when usually he avoids me.

He's semi-shifted, his teeth and claws lengthened. When I was a child, this worked to intimidate me up until that moment he hurt Eyin. I am taller, stronger, much more skilled than he had ever been even in his prime. He has let years of indulgence soften him and dull his abilities.

Konai or not, my kin or not, I will kill him if he dares attack me.

Sensing the impending destruction, Ronan speaks up.

"My dearest Konai, there's no need for you to get worked up." Ronan's tone is cajoling as one would speak to their lover when they're being unreasonable. "Perhaps Theron only seeks to prevent you from worry. You have had much to drink. You should get some rest."

Ronan rubs Aphat's shoulder in a comforting, intimate gesture. Sometimes I wonder if there isn't more to their friendship.

Aphat was married once and never remarried after the Konai sa's abrupt death. I have heard rumours about Aphat's proclivities. His choices when he visits whorehouses whose silence he believes he's bought. How these choices often skew more male than female. How Ronan often accompanies him, too.

Aphat glares at me before he retreats completely to his primary form. Then he turns and strides out the door.

How is that he and I share blood? Why do I serve beneath a being like that? Why is Andrasar in the hands of someone like him?

"I've heard something troubling, Ronan," I say as soon as Aphat is gone. "Are you killing Andrasari under allegations they support the human rebellions without first giving them a fair trial?"

He scowls and doesn't respond right away.

"We all have our jobs to do, Theron," he says finally, tapping his desk's surface. "While you're the one tasked to keep Andrasar running efficiently, I am the one who keeps it safe."

"You are not doing your duty if you're instigating war," I say, frowning at him. "What do you think will happen if you keep this up? There are far-reaching consequences to your actions."

He sneers. "Indeed, there are consequences and it is fear. I want the Andrasari to understand there's nothing to gain but death from supporting these vile cretins inhabiting our soil."

"What you are doing is breeding resentment in the Andrasari. Then a fight that was once so easy to squash will become much harder." I pause. "I've also received word you imprisoned slaves within the Andrak, my *zevyet* among them."

"Is that the true reason why you returned so quickly, Theron?" Ronan asks, unsettling me. "Did you cancel your important meeting to come running to save your little human slave?"

Disturbed by what's unfolding, I advance toward him. When did it become like this? Ronan might have always been Aphat's friend, but he never treated me like an enemy.

Now, I'm not sure anymore. I dislike that his words hold truth in them too.

"You are implying something dangerous, Ronan," I say, my tone low and filled with a warning.

"I heard about what happened at that mining plant in Vak. The riot that got out of hand because you let your slave speak for you. Instead of destroying the disrespectful humans who tried to fight, you spared their lives because of your *zevyet*'s pleas." Ronan's gaze is dark and filled with disgust. "I fear your focus is being compromised, Theron. Your values eroding because of a human's poisonous nature."

I grab the front of his jacket and drag him close, ready to kill him for speaking the truth. But he doesn't flinch away from me.

"We've had a long and successful friendship, Ronan. It would be a shame for us to lose it due to your disrespectful tongue."

"I apologize. I misspoke," he says, his tone unapologetic. He smiles with triumph. A chill curls along my spine at how similar he looks to Aphat now. Disgusted, I release him. "You asked me to investigate your attack and I did. The human I have imprisoned aided in the theft of the weapons."

Seela's pleas of the human's innocence and her implication that Ronan set this up sounds in my head. I didn't believe her then but the barely concealed disdain in Ronan's gaze makes me doubt myself.

Why would Ronan use this human as a scapegoat unless he had something to hide? The dark thought that maybe Ronan organized my attack manifests. Yet when you've known someone for a long time and have considered them your ally for just as long, it's not a welcome thought to question their loyalty.

"How do you know this?" I ask him. "Have you tracked his collar's locations near the armory around the date of my attack?"

"I have not because it is unnecessary. His possession of the key is proof of his guilt."

"If he's guilty he would not have kept it."

"Why do you defend the human?" Ronan sneers. He seems angry, as if he'd not expected me to question his decisions.

"This is not justice. You do a disservice to me for punishing another while the real culprit of my attack still roams free."

He releases a long-suffering sigh.

"I didn't want to disclose this but you leave me no choice," he says. "The Konai feels it unnecessary I continue in the investigation of your attack, especially now that we've found a suspect. He would prefer I publicly execute the human for the crime and turn my attention to matters of importance."

I am unsurprised Aphat deems an assault that almost claimed my life an 'unimportant matter'.

"This will not end well, Ronan," I say. "If you kill this human who the others believe are innocent, this will be the catalyst that brings another war to our gates."

"I act on the word of the Konai." His tone is obstinate, his eyes gleaming with excitement. "Tomorrow, the human will pay the price as an example to the others of the consequences of defying us. If they want war, let there be war. And then I will kill them all."

Chapter Thirteen

Theron

The courtyard of the Andrak is packed with humans the morning of the human's execution.

Andrasari guards surround them to keep them contained. Seela and I stand beneath the Andrak's awning, outside of the crowd.

In the center is a platform. Atop it the condemned human is tied to a pole.

"You don't have to be here," I tell Seela quietly.

She hasn't said a word to me on her own since the night before. I've often been irritated by her chattiness but now her silence discomforts me.

She only speaks when she is spoken to and avoids my gaze. When she looks at me, it's with an unfocused stare like if she's willing herself to pretend I don't exist.

"I have to for Xia, *zevyena*," she says, her tone devoid of any emotion.

It should make me happy that she's finally behaving the way she is supposed to, but I'm far from it. There's this dark unpleasant thing coalescing in my chest. A variety of emotions that are dangerous to unpack because they go directly against my ideologies.

There's the guilt that the human tied to the pole above is losing his life indirectly because of me.

There's the anger that despite all my power, I'm still unable to put an end to what's about to happen.

And worst of all is the cold understanding that once this human loses his life, Seela might never again look at me the way she did the night before.

Which should be a good thing. What we almost did was a mistake of enormous proportions. What we almost did shouldn't have even be considered.

My thoughts return to the present when Ronan climbs onto the platform. High above in one of the Andrak's balconies stands Aphat with his guards, presiding over the affair.

"Today, I will teach you all a valuable lesson," begins Ronan, addressing the humans. "This human before you has been found guilty of thievery and facilitating a group assault upon our most excellent Nai Theron Visclaud. For these crimes, the Konai has ordered that this scum be sentenced to death. A death you shall all witness. He is to be made an example of the consequences of defying and rebelling against your *zevyena*." He turns to the human. "Do you have anything to say for yourself? Do you repent of your crimes?"

Angry mutterings spread throughout the crowd, their features contorted with hate. A tense energy thickens the air and as if the guards are aware of it, they withdraw their weapons. Despite their strength and training, they are Unshifted Andrasari and the humans outnumber them.

"I love you, Xia," says the human, his voice uneven from emotion, his purpling, misshapen face glistening with tears. "In my absence, may Kahafura continue to protect you, bless you with happiness, and the strength to forgive those who hurt you."

Preferring humans to beg for their lives, Ronan sneers and hits the human over the head. Humans in the crowd cry out at this, but grow silent when he shifts into his dragon.

His large metal-grey form inhabits the skies. The gust from his wings pushes a few of the humans back, his tail snapping to and fro like a vicious whip.

He roars, calling forth the fire from his belly.

He has no need to be so dramatic to kill one human.

He has no need to kill this human at all.

The human on the platform faces his impending execution bravely. He doesn't beg for mercy even as Ronan lowers his head and breathes fire on him.

I've heard countless humans scream as I burned them alive and I've always taken satisfaction in the sound.

For the first time, I take no joy in a human's suffering.

Clenching my fists I endure the terrible wailing. Even in extreme pain, he does not beg.

"Don't look," I tell Seela.

I reach for her to turn her away because I don't want this image forever ingrained in her mind. She wrenches away before I can touch her. Her eyes are shiny with tears, the fire's glow dancing in them.

She doesn't look away. She takes it all in. She will remember this moment forever. She will remember that even though it was not me who burned the human male alive, I was still responsible because of who I am.

The human's screaming comes to an abrupt end and Ronan returns to the platform, naked in his primary form. The fire still burns on the pole but all is silent.

The energy of the crowd is darker and tenser than before. If Ronan senses it, he doesn't seem to care. He smirks at the furious faces surrounding him, triumphant in his act. He opens his mouth, no doubt to say more that would rub salt in the wound he's just torn wide open.

A shout erupts and a human female launches herself onto the platform.

"*Vi ocir eus oce!*" she screams. It's one of Andrasari's oldest and darkest motto popularized by my war-mongering grandfather when he was the Konai.

You kill or die.

Kill or be killed.

She's quicker than Ronan anticipated, her rage fuelling her movements. She tackles Ronan to the ground, a knife in her fist arcing through the air as she stabs him repeatedly in the neck and chest.

Andrasari guards flood the platform and yank the human off Ronan. They end her life with a violent twist of her neck.

Dragon's Captive

Anarchy erupts as fighting ensues. I'm caught between duty to subdue the crowd and the need to protect Seela.

I choose the latter by grabbing her hand and hurrying her toward one of the Andrak's entrances. There's havoc inside the Andrak too, the crowd of humans swarming everywhere as they chant at the top of their voices, "*Vi ocir eus oce!*"

"Stay here," I order when we're in my quarters. "Don't let anyone inside. Human or Andrasari. It's not safe until I have everything under control."

She nods silently and I leave.

Ronan is no longer on the platform, but there's a large pool of blood on its surface. It's a possibility that he's dead because as much as a Shifted Rur can withstand grave injuries, we are still fallible to an attack on our vital organs. Ronan was stabbed in the chest. Maybe the blade found his heart.

Of course, Aphat is gone and no longer presiding over the violent aftermath. Using the collars to shock the humans into submission is out of the question because it would hurt Seela too.

There are a few *draki* burning humans alive and I order them to spare the humans' lives and corral them instead. Some of the humans escape and I don't bother giving chase.

Once the remainder are subdued, Unshifted guards arrest them and drag them away to the prison cells

Chapter Fourteen

Theron

It takes the remainder of the day to have everything in order.

By the time I visit Eyin to ascertain Ronan's condition, evening has fallen.

"He'll live," says Eyin quietly. "He'll be recovered and on his feet in a few days."

This news should give me relief but instead, I feel nothing. As I stare at Ronan lying unconscious on Eyin's table, all I feel is anger for what he's done.

When I was a child, he was the one I held as a role model because of his ability to stand up against Aphat. We were supposed to be on the same side. The one working toward bettering Andrasar in spite of Aphat's persistence in driving it to the ground.

Dragon's Captive

When had things changed?

Eyin gathers medical supplies in a bag as if in preparation to leave.

I frown. "Where are you going?"

"I have to tend to the humans who were injured in the fight," she says.

"That would be a foolish thing to do, Eyin. They will not react kindly to an Andrasari tending to their wounds."

She purses her lips. "But they need my help—"

"No." I say the words harsher than I'd intended and she deflates. I relent, upset with myself. "Not yet. I need to make them aware they've been given a second chance despite what they did. That they will get no other if they persist in their disobedience."

"That's not like you at all. You never give second chances."

"Ronan took the life of a human in the hope of starting a war. I want to make sure I nip it in the bud."

I don't look at her when I speak and for that reason she knows that's not the entire truth. She peers at me, her intelligent mind coming to the right conclusion in mere seconds.

"Are you doing this because of Seela?" she asks.

"Sparing the lives of the humans are of no benefit to her."

"No, but you want her. I saw the way you were looking at her that first day you brought her here. You know that if you kill them she'll never want anything to do with you."

"Don't be ridiculous, Eyin. I can't want a human."

"You tell yourself you 'can't' but that doesn't mean you 'don't'." She smiles at my scowl. "What an ironic situation to be in, Theron Visclaud, the great despiser of all humans."

"There's more to the irony," I say quietly. "She is my fire's half."

Eyin's eyes widen before she throws her head back with a laugh. It's not the reaction I expected but for such a horrific day, it's good to hear the sound of my sister's amusement.

When her humour dies away, she becomes somber as she hugs me.

"I'm happy for you, Theron, because you've found something so many wish they could find. But you've built a wall so high around yourself, blocking you from what's yours."

Unsure of how to respond, I ruffle the top of her head like I used to when we were children. Squawking in protest, she slaps at my hand and shoos me away.

Dragon's Captive

When I return home, I find Seela standing by one of the large windows that overlooks the city below us. She doesn't acknowledge my presence and I hesitate. But I refuse to cower from her.

"Seela."

"Yes, *zevyena*?" she answers, but she doesn't look at me.

I scowl at that. Yesterday, it's exactly what I demanded her to call me. In this moment I know she's using it as a shield, as a way to distance herself from me. Just as I would call her 'human' or 'slave' when thoughts of having her beneath me became too prominent in my head.

"I am not the one who killed the human today," I say. "Your anger is misguided."

She makes a sound of derision. "'The human'. That's what we all are to you. A collective word with no individuality because it's easier to hate us and mistreat us that way." Finally she meets my gaze, her eyes shining with anger. "He was a person with a name. *Shihong*. Not just 'human'."

Every single bit of me aches to reach for her, hold her, and comfort her, but I know she won't accept it. Not from me. Not when I represent her misery. I shouldn't either. That would be dangerous.

"I promised Xia," she says staring out the window again, shaking her head. "I promised her I'd get him free." She pauses. "I guess he is in death. Free from mistreatment and injustice."

I should be happy she looks like this, sounds like this. A broken human, her shoulders hung low in defeat, her voice laced with nothing but bitter resignation. This is what has brought me satisfaction for years in the humans. That look in their eyes when they realize there's no hope left for them.

There's none of that now where I stand. Instead, guilt presses on my chest, and along with it comes a doubt in myself and my beliefs. Something I've never questioned before.

It's ridiculous how this weak, tiny creature makes me feel so minuscule, makes me question the truth of what I've been fed all these years. If I can see her for what she is—something good and honest—would it be a challenge to see more of her kind in a positive light?

These thoughts discomfort me. They are too foreign for me to welcome right now.

"You seem to have fantastical expectations despite knowing the dark reality of your existence." I step closer. "Would it ease your disappointment if I told you that I tried? I tried to have his life spared even though he was a suspect in a crime that almost took my life. Even though I never spare the life of someone who tries to harm me."

"Then why am I here? I stabbed you. Why don't you tie me to the pole and burn me alive too?"

"Because you are different."

Her anger dissipates, replaced by surprise. She regards me for a moment in silence while I stand in regret that I uttered the words.

"The only thing that's different about me is that I was stupid enough to save your life. Stupid enough...*overconfident* enough to think that doing so would change the way you view my kind. I should have left you for dead." Her dark-brown eyes flash with anger. "I should have turned around and continued on my way far away from you."

I move toward her. She retreats until there's nowhere to go, the window's glass pressed against her back. And still, I occupy her space until there's not much left between us.

"You should have, then we both would have died in blissful ignorance of each other." I tilt her chin and lower my face to hers. "Yet you stayed and cursed us both."

This time I don't hesitate. I take her lips against mine and my dragon storms within me, restless and demanding that I take more.

She fights me of course, because Seela is my fire's half and, like me, never gives into anything easily. She pushes against my chest and wrenches her face away. I grab her wrists and pin them above her head, and she immediately squirms against my grasp.

She ceases her struggle when she realizes she can't free herself from my hold.

I'm stronger than her, bigger than her, unyielding against her pliant delicateness.

She is my antithesis.

I am the darkness that will consume her glorious light.

She breathes deeply, her eyes shiny with dislike and outrage. Even when she hates me, she is the most fucking beautiful thing I've ever seen and I want her so badly it's like a deep, persistent ache in some intangible part of me.

Her body heat has risen, the scent of her arousal eroding my usual steely grip on logic. My resistance to this thing between us has met its death. The beast inside me does not care about consequence.

It only cares that it has the thing it desires most in its clutches and it intends to feast.

Chapter Fifteen

Seela

It isn't just Theron before me anymore.

It's that dark monster that lives inside him, too.

It's night and the only light around us is from the city below. Theron looms over me like a shadow in the gloom but I still see his face. I still see the way his eyes gleam golden and fiery with a hunger that steals my breath, and I know that he's going to consume me where we stand.

I won't let him. I won't give in to him even if my nipples are hard points seeking his attention and between my legs is slick, burning for his touch.

I'm still recovering from his first kiss when he accosts me with another one. He angles his head to the side, his tongue swiping at the seam of my lips before slipping into my mouth.

Lust wraps me up in its heat, smothering me the moment his tongue curls against mine. But the voice inside my head, the one that's filled with good sense and foresight, screams at me to fight again.

Don't give in.

Trying to free my hands from his hold, I twist away from his kiss. That leaves my neck exposed. Theron drags his lips across my jaw and latches onto the skin below my ear.

The damp heat of his mouth and tongue inspires a tightening sensation between my legs and pulls a whimper from lips. His free hand finds the tie on my slave's robe and loosens it with a yank. The ends of my robe hang open, baring me in my underwear.

Heat floods my face in anger and in mortification. Only one other male has seen me like this, but it's been so long ago that this moment feels like the first time all over again.

The look on Theron's face as his gaze scorches my skin frightens me with its intensity. I'm the meat set before a wild, hungry animal who has been chained too long and is now released.

It's futile to tug free from his hold. His hand might as well be a metal clamp around my wrists. I've gained strength working in the bakery hefting heavy sacks of baking product, but I'm like a tiny bird in Theron's grasp.

"Are you a virgin, Seela?" he asks suddenly, his voice is deeper and rougher. When I don't answer, he gives me a dark smile. "I suppose it doesn't matter. As far as I'm concerned, I will be your first and your only."

"Touch me and you die, Andrasari," I spit.

"Your threats are empty and pointless." He pushes his face close to mine, his voice a rasp. He slips a finger just under the edge of my bra, sliding it so his finger caresses the undersides of my breasts. "You're going to love what I'm about to do to you, Seela. You're going to beg for my cock, and when I've buried it deep inside you, you're going to cry for more of it while I'm fucking you."

"You should throw away all that arrogance and remember your morals, Andrasari," I say in mocking tones.

My heart races, my lungs desperate for air. His filthy promise is too loud, drowning out the rational voice.

I inhale sharply when he shoves up the stretchy material of my bra, revealing my breasts to his ravenous gaze. He cups one in his big, rough hand.

Pinching my nipple between two fingers, he tugs it. My jaw slackens as my treacherous body moves on its own, my chest arching toward his contact.

"According to you, I have no morals," he says, his tone equally mocking as he continues to pinch and fondle my flesh. "According to you, I am the hateful bastard with no regard for you and your kind." He bends his head so his lips move against my ear. "But what does that make you…" His hand slides from my breast, skimming my ribcage, inching past my navel. I squirm when his fingertips tickle the skin just above the top edge of my underwear. "…when you desire someone like me?"

A traitor who wants her enemy's touch.

A traitor who moans shamefully when it's received.

Theron's fingers slips into my underwear, his fingers sliding lower, parting me. He presses against my tight bud and I lift up onto my toes. I squeeze my eyes shut, and my lips too so that I don't let out the cry rising in my throat.

"Widen your legs, Seela," he growls. His fingertips design lazy circles on my sensitive flesh. I press my legs tighter together defiantly, constricting his hand.

"I'm not giving in to you," I say, but my voice lacks conviction.

A triumphant smile curves his lips. It's infuriating. I want to slap it off his face.

"You're so beautiful when you're stubborn."

He releases my wrists at the same time he grabs hold of my underwear and yanks it down my thighs. Without thinking, I spread them to let the scrap of cloth fall freely to the floor. Theron seizes that opportunity to wedge his fingers between my legs.

His fingers curve up and invade my channel at the same time his mouth comes crashing down on mine again. My resolve has weakened considerably, assaulted by the things he's doing to my body.

When I return Theron's kiss, I do it angrily, fiercely.

Just because I'm finally giving in doesn't mean I enjoy it.

Which is a lie because I do.

And I hate myself for it.

Hate him for it.

Yet I don't want him any less.

What we're doing feels inevitable. Fighting against it is like trying to contain a roaring fire with your hands.

His thick fingers fuck me as his tongue dominates mine. I grip the front of his jacket to push him away. Instead I open my legs wider for him. I fist his jacket and pull him closer as he swallows my whimpers of pleasure like if my capitulation gives him life.

He breaks our kiss, his breath warm on my lips. He palms my breast, rolling my nipple between his fingers. A wet sound comes from where his other fingers manipulate me to his will.

Each stroke makes me tighter, makes my breathing come faster, makes me lift my hips in desperation for the finish that his fingers promise me.

My body is pulled taut and straining.

He is right that he is my first. I've explored my own body but I've never felt anything like this before. Never been touched like this by anyone. Maybe he's right, too, that he will be my only.

But Theron slows to a torturous pace that makes me tremble with frustration

"Theron..." I pant. I don't recognize that voice. That can't be me sounding so desperate. "You bastard..."

"I can't give you what you want if you insult me." He squeezes my breast and pushes a third finger into me, stretching me so that I cry out and rise up on my tiptoes. His hand must be drenched by how aroused I am. "But I can if you beg for it."

I can't think straight anymore. I just want release.

"You want me to say please?"

"No, that's not enough. You can do better than that."

"Then... please..." I grind my hips down on him. "...Please fuck me."

He withdraws his hand from me to remove his jacket. Once he's finally rid of his pants, he snares me around the waist and drags me to the floor.

His mouth covers mine in a hungry kiss I return with as much fervour. I slide my hands down his arms, caressing the even ridges of the scales on his skin.

He shudders at my touch and I delight in the low groan of pleasure he makes in the back of his throat. I didn't know an Andrasari grew aroused from their scales being touched.

My head spins at the speed at which we're moving. One moment we were arguing over one thing, the next we're on the floor tangled together.

What we're doing is wrong, forbidden even. I am a human slave and he is Andrasari royalty. If we're discovered like this, I will be killed and maybe Theron too for violating the ideologies of his people.

We're supposed to be enemies, so how did we end up here? Why is it that when he touches me it doesn't feel wrong at all? Maybe he's right that we've both been cursed.

He's a mountain of hard, hot flesh between my legs and bearing down on me. His cock lays on my belly, rigid and warm. The weight of it... the length of it... I try not to tremble from the fear of being unable to accommodate him.

He puts his hand to my neck and there's a gentle click. The collar slackens and falls away.

"I don't want a slave," he says as he angles his length against my slick entrance and slides into me. "I want you."

I've sunk to the darkness with him and I realize that I don't want to return to the light if I can't have him with me.

His lips hover over mine, swallowing my gasp as he fills me, stretches me. There's so much of him, almost too much. He has to withdraw and shove into me in order to fully enter me.

When he does, my back curves away from the floor. My walls tighten around him, but there's no yield, no softness. His cock is hard and unforgiving. It's going to destroy me.

And I'm going to love every single second of my destruction by this powerful dragon prince.

He releases a pained grunt as he thrusts into me. Puffs of his warm breath tickles my collarbone. That coil of pleasure he'd already wound inside me restarts its spiral. He's not gentle. He props himself up on his elbows as he takes me rough and with animalistic desperation.

I'm heady that I made this strong-willed male lose his restraint. Around others, he's reserved to the point of cold. But with me, he's a beast possessed by lust and determination to claim me as his.

"Theron..." I gasp, shivering beneath him, my fingernails scraping down his broad, muscular back. I'm held in the grips of my climax, overrun by pleasure and heat sweeping through my body.

Swearing, a groan of pleasure rumbling in his chest, Theron comes inside me. His flesh throbs, filling me with his seed. I clamp down on him tightly, hoping to milk every last drop inside my body.

An incredible wave of sensation and tingling warmth sweeps through me. My heart gallops as I'm suddenly filled with a burst of energy. It's different than an orgasm but it feels just as amazing.

He nuzzles my neck, his hand gliding along my hip and thigh in a caress that's far gentler than what we just did.

"You're mine, always mine, Seela." He says it softly like if he meant to keep the words in his head and has mistakenly said them out loud.

"Yes," I whisper, too terrified of how true the words are to say them any louder. "Yes, Theron, I'm yours."

Chapter Sixteen

Seela

Sleeping with your enemy shouldn't be an invisible line that you might accidentally cross.

It should be a tall fence covered in poisonous spikes to deter you from climbing it.

It had felt so right when Theron's hands caressed me, when his lips were against mine, when he rasped in my ear that he wanted me, when he brought me to levels of pleasure I'd never known existed.

In that moment, we had forgotten who we were supposed to be to each other.

Of course, after it was over we were forced to remember.

I wallow in guilt. However, I don't regret because that would mean I would've made a different choice if given a second chance. I wouldn't. I still would have let him kiss me and take me on his floor and relish every single second of it.

Worst of all, I would let him do it again.

And it's for this reason why the guilt tightens my chest and weighs down my shoulders.

I really am a traitor. To myself and to my people.

While Xia was still in prison mourning the execution of her father by an Andrasari, I willingly let their prince claim my body as his. Several days later, his touch is still a phantom on my skin.

I try to pretend that all is normal. That I'm just another *zevyet* trapped in service to her *zevyena*. That when I close my eyes I don't see the hunger in his gaze when he loomed over me. That I don't hear his moan as he came inside me.

That I didn't mean it when I said I was his.

However, if I thought Theron was a bastard prior to what happened between us the night of Shihong's execution, he really lives up to the name now.

The wall he usually has surrounding him is thicker, higher, and colder than before. He either harshly criticizes the things I do for him or rewards me with chilly silence.

His inability to look at me, and his avoidance from being in the same room as me for too long is proof enough that even though I don't regret, he certainly does.

Seated in the main room, I try to pay attention to the book I'm reading. He's in his office and he's speaking. Maybe he's in a meeting. His angry tones intrigue me. I abandon my book and draw closer to the closed door as his muffled voice becomes more coherent.

"...burning villages. Now they will fashion weapons from all of that stolen Rurium... That's because you underestimated their intelligence. They've become coordinated—hold for one moment. I've an unwelcome audience."

Oh, dear. I forgot Andrasari beings have that pesky ability to smell you from far away.

I'm about to hurry away when his door abruptly opens and he catches me.

We hold each other's stare. I'm frozen where I stand, my brain at a loss for words.

"Is the rebellion getting stronger?" I finally ask.

"That's none of your concern, human," he says coldly. "Get back to whatever it is you were doing and stay away from this door."

"We're back to 'human' now?"

Goddess above, I need a trade. I need a new pair of lips because mine is defective and clearly has a

Dragon's Captive

penchant for getting me into trouble.

Theron regards me in amazement like if he can't believe I dared speak those words. Frankly, I'm pretty amazed myself. I swallow and force myself to speak hurriedly.

"I just want to keep up to date on what's going on. I haven't seen anything beyond these walls ever since… ever since Shihong's execution." Heat floods my face as that ever present memory of what we did *after* Shihong's execution jumps into remembrance with ease.

He stares at me in silence and I resist the urge to drop my gaze. Finally, a dark look of resolution crosses his features. Like if he's come to some sort of decision.

"You need to leave."

I hate myself that instead of feeling joy at his words, I feel panic.

"Are you releasing me?"

"Yes, I'm relieving you of your duties as my *zevyet*," he says, his voice emotionless. "You will serve as a slave within the Andrak's as well as reside in the areas designated for your kind. Gather whatever items you deem important from your room and find your way there."

"Why?"

"I am your master," he sneers. "You will do what I say without question, slave."

He has said these words to me before countless times and they've left me unfazed. This time, they're like a punch to the gut, winding me from the shock that it hurts.

I turn around before he can see the tears because I feel ridiculous for crying. Wasting my tears on him is bad enough, much less to let this bastard see them.

"There's nothing important here for me that I need," I say coldly. "Please give me access to the doors so that I can leave right away."

He sounds the command to his security system. With squared shoulders, I march out of his quarters without a clue as to where I need to go. I take the lift to the lowest level and it's only after I've stepped into the gloomy corridor do I realize I had the opportunity to escape.

I've been a caged creature for so long that even when my master no longer wants me, I still obey his orders.

Eyin comes into view before I can head back into the lift and escape this place.

"Why are you here, Seela?" she asks.

"I made a mistake."

Dragon's Captive

Let her believe I mean that I got off on the wrong floor. She doesn't know that the mistake I made was the day I ran toward the dragon roaring in the forest so long ago.

She gives me a strange look. "Do you want me to lead you back to Theron's—"

"No." I say sharply. Then I soften my voice and give her a tight smile. "It's not necessary. I am no longer Nai Theron's *zevyet*. I am now in service to the Andrak."

She stares at me for a while and frowns. "He still hasn't told you?"

"Told me what?"

She shakes her head, flashing a quick smile.

"Just speaking out loud. Nothing to concern you."

I don't believe her. As friendly as Eyin is, she is still Theron's sister. If she's anything like her brother whose temperaments change as often as the wind changes direction, it would be foolish to challenge her words.

"Since you don't seem to know what to do with yourself, do you want to work with me in the infirmary for the day?" she asks. "There are still many injured humans from the fight that occurred after Shihong's execution." Her features turn somber. "His daughter is helping as much as she can, too."

Xia. That night I'd stupidly promised her I'd help free her father was the last time I'd seen her. I'm reluctant to face her now.

Leaving her without at least seeing her once more is the coward's way out. I need to apologize for giving her false hope only for her to have it brutally crushed.

"Yes, I'd like to help," I say to Eyin.

She leads me away to the infirmary.

Chapter Seventeen

Seela

Rows of beds filled with infirm humans populate the infirmary.

The male Andrasari I saw my first time here, peers at a console's holographic screen that's littered with indecipherable text. He's so engrossed in his work, he seems unaware of our entrance.

Standing beside a bed, Xia leans over a resting human some distance away. Cloth in hand, she wipes their forehead. She lifts her head from her task, glancing at Eyin before settling her gaze on me.

My chest feels tight and heavy with dread and guilt.

"Can I speak with Xia quickly before I begin?" I ask Eyin.

With a nod, she leaves me to check on a patient.

What a difference she is to her brother. Most of the time when I make a request of Theron, the first word to his lips is 'no'.

Making my way over to Xia, I push thoughts of Theron aside.

"How are you?"

It's such a trite question to ask, but I don't know where to start. Her brown eyes don't hold any hostility. Her lips curve up a bit and I relax marginally.

"I'm glad to see you're well, Seela," she says, avoiding my question.

I decide to launch right into what I want to say. "Xia, I'm so sorry—"

She raises a hand. "Don't be. You meant well and I believe that you tried, but it was too late to save him." There's a waver in her voice as she speaks. "It's my fault he died, anyway."

"It wasn't your fault," I say forcefully. I hate that she blames herself for something like this. It's hard enough to lose a loved one, let alone carry the burden of guilt that they died because of you.

I would know because I share her experience. If it weren't for me, Ikkon would still be alive today. But because he chose to treat me as someone of value, he lost his life.

I lower my voice. "Ronan set it all up to have a scapegoat to torture. He loved nothing more than to kill humans. But he can't hurt anymore now that he's dead."

"The bastard didn't die, his Shifted blood saved him." Xia's hands tighten over the cloth in her hand, her voice like a chilled blade. "He's already on his feet killing even more humans. See these?" She points at the collar around her neck. It's a new one made of Rurium steel, a sinister gleam on its black coat. "It doesn't just shock you like before, it explodes." Even though her face is a mask of fury, her eyes shine with unshed tears. "I saw them exhibit it on Jogen when he tried to escape."

It's the most horrific thing I've ever heard. My skin crawls. An awful sensation coils along my spine at the thought that Theron had a hand in this gruesome method to subjugate my people.

Xia's gaze darts to my neck then focuses on me.

"Why aren't you wearing one of the new collars? It was mandatory of all humans."

"Theron—Nai Theron never told me about it. He has kept me chained away from everything since..." I don't bother finishing the sentence. I know she knows when I'm talking about.

"I guess he doesn't want to see you explode into several bloody pieces."

There's something in her tone that makes me nervous, as well as her intent stare that is gradually becoming suspicious.

I smile tightly at her. "I'm glad to see you, Xia. I should probably speak with Eyin now to see how I can help—"

Xia grabs my hand suddenly, her voice an accusatory whisper.

"You're his lover, aren't you?"

"Of course not," I say, but I've spoken too quickly and my voice is too high. Even to my own ears, I hear how false my words sound. "I'm not even his *zevyet* anymore."

Her grip tightens, her gaze feral. "You're lying. That night we all got imprisoned, he cut his trip short and came back to free you, to protect you. When you told me you would help set my father free, you knew you had his ear, didn't you? You knew that you could convince him to do it because you mean more to him than just a slave."

"Obviously that's not true because it didn't work. Your father still died," I say in angry, hushed tones. I wrench my hand free from her grasp. "You're mistaken, Xia. I don't mean anything to the Nai of Andrasar."

"What was the favour you did for him, Seela?" she asks abruptly. When I don't answer right away, she snarls at me. "What did you do?"

Don't tell her.

But the truth still leaves me.

"I saved his life."

I watch as she adds everything up in her head. The attack on Theron's life that Ronan mentioned at Shihong's execution. The one her father was wrongfully condemned for. I see the way she looks at me. I see the word in her eyes before it's formed on her lips.

"Traitor," she spits. "You've not only helped the enemy against your own people, you're sleeping with him too." She vibrates with rage. "I'm going to kill Ronan and Aphat for taking my father's life. I'm especially going to make sure your lover is dead too."

"Xia, doing something like that—"

"Is everything all right here?" comes Eyin's concerned voice. She frowns at Xia. Did she hear her threats?

Xia doesn't answer. She shoves me out of her way and storms out of the infirmary.

Dragon's Captive

Standing beside the bed of the patient Xia treated, I stare at the cloth she abandoned on the floor. I feel as limp and wrung out as that cloth.

I'm going to be one of the most hated individuals in the Andrak once Xia has told the other humans what I've done. Maybe even more hated than Aphat, Ronan and Theron combined.

"I can't stay here." I didn't mean to speak the words out loud. Caught up in my self-pity, I forget that Eyin is still close enough to hear me.

"Where will you go if you were to leave?" she asks softly.

"Far away," I say, looking up at her. "Far, far away from here."

She gives a short nod as if my answer is sufficient. She moves closer and puts a comforting hand on my shoulder.

"I will come for you tonight. Be ready." Then she pulls away from me with a smile while my open lips are still parted from shock. "Now let's get to work healing our patients."

What I lack significantly in medical experience, Eyin makes up for it with patience as she guides me. It is evident how much she loves her work. I find myself as envious of her passion as I am amazed by the things she can do.

After the abysmal encounters I had with Theron and Xia, I didn't expect to find any joy in this day, but there is something deeply satisfying and rewarding helping the patients in the infirmary.

All my life, all I knew was baking. I didn't have a talent for it like Ikkon did. I became good at it through years of practice. I never envisioned any grand career for myself because humans aren't afforded that luxury.

I was content with the knowledge that I would spend the rest of my years at the bakery. It never even entered my mind that someday Ikkon wouldn't be around to be my guardian. That the bakery wouldn't always be my home.

But working with Eyin opens my eyes to possibilities, to dangerous hope that I've finally found something that connects with me. Especially when Eyin praises the tiniest things I do and proclaims me a 'natural'.

"With training, you can become an excellent medic," she says, genuine excitement in her eyes. Her compliment is like the sun and water combined, and I am the dying plant finding new life as it's showered on me. I wilt again when she adds in a quieter voice: "But I can't train if you won't be here. Any second thoughts?"

My resolution waivers, but I shake my head.

"No."

When curfew rolls around, she tells me to stay in one of the beds in the infirmary.

The time seems to crawl as I lay awake waiting for her. Whenever I close my eyes all I can see is Theron's face twisted with fury when he realizes I'm gone.

He won't care. He's already cast me aside. He didn't even threaten me about running away when I left this morning. As far as he's concerned, I no longer exist to him.

This thought hurts me more than it should so I do my best to forget about him.

Eventually, Eyin comes for me.

"Here," she says, handing me a bag similar to the one I owned before I came here. "Some food stuff that should last you awhile."

The Andrak is deadly silent as she hurries me along. My heart thuds in my chest, certain we will be discovered. A part of me harbours distrust in Eyin, but I focus on keeping up with her swift pace.

At the end of one gloomy corridor, Eyin presses her hand against what I assume is solid wall. But it slides away revealing a cavern of absolute darkness.

"This tunnel leads past the Andrak walls to an alley in the city. There's a holomap in the bag so you don't get lost."

She closes her eyes and holds out her hand. A bloom of golden light in the shape of a ball forms in her palms. It's a *safur*. Bits of her energy transformed into light and mild heat.

Ikkon would make them for me when I was a child to entertain me. I didn't know Unshifted Andrasari could create them too.

The golden light of the *safur* shines on her face as she indicates I take it.

"You should go now before that dies," she says, pointing at the *safur*. "It's very dark in the tunnels."

I look into the yawning blackness. It's frightening, but it's also my escape. Then I meet Eyin's gaze again.

"Why are you helping me?"

She points at her cheek where her scar is hidden by her hair.

"It was Aphat who gave this to me. I called him cruel for killing and enslaving humans when it all began and he slapped me with Shifted fingers. Theron tried to kill him and he almost succeeded despite being so young." She smiled as if it's a fond memory when in fact it is depressing. "But I begged him not to because Aphat was our only family after our parents died. Aphat continued on to massacre and enslave even more humans. So, you see, humans' misery all rests on my shoulders. Had I left Theron to finish the job, Aphat would be dead and Theron would be the Konai today."

"It still wouldn't have changed the fate of humans. Theron hates all of us."

"Except one." She smiles. "Sometimes, that's all you need. Just one to change the fate of the many."

Chapter Eighteen

Theron

Past midnight while I doze in my office, the tracker embedded in Seela's collar fires off an alarm to my implant.

She's gone beyond the boundaries of the Andrak.

I'm awake and on my feet in seconds, ready to hunt her down and drag her back to my quarters.

It's only after I've stormed out of my office do I remember that I shouldn't give chase.

I shouldn't care.

This is what I wanted. I sent her away from me because as much as I despise Ronan for saying it, he is right.

Seela poisoned my thoughts, chipped away at the beliefs I've held on to for years. As the human

Dragon's Captive

rebellions are at their strongest and getting out of hand, I question my actions. Instead of killing those I've found guilty of disobedience, I have them imprisoned.

Of course, Ronan undermines me by executing them. Aphat has grant him more power than I possess and it has changed him into an unrecognizable being.

Since he was attacked by the human, Ronan's viciousness and hatred has magnified. He conjures up various gruesome ways to destroy the humans—his latest invention a collar that explodes and kills the human who wears it.

It's a step too far and I know that even some Andrasari who were die-hard supporters of the enslavement of humans think this too. As Ronan continues to kill his own kind in a misguided quest for compliance, more Andrasari join the rebellion.

The fight grows stronger, the human's voices are louder, and they're finally being heard.

I stand in front of my door for a long time, my dragon restless and angry that my fire's half has ran away. It demands I go after her and properly claim her with the bite, sealing her as my mate. This way, she will never want to leave me again.

No, I have to let her go. While it isn't safe for her beyond the walls of the Andrak, bringing her here might jeopardize her further. The slaves within the Andrak have been spared because they serve the Andrasari who serve the Konai, but in time, Ronan will kill them next.

So I return to my office, my body tense with anger. I am furious with myself that as a being with so much power, I am still powerless.

Is it truly powerlessness or cowardice?

Ronan and Aphat needs to be stopped and yet I do nothing. Seela needs to be reclaimed and protected, yet I hide away in my office. I am set before a crossroad and reluctant to make a choice because I fear the consequences.

I don't get any sleep for the rest of the night. The following day, my mood is as black as my scales in my dragon form.

It isn't improved when the Overseer of Tarro region sends me a curt missive that Tarro wished to end trade ties with Andrasar should the persecution of humans and Rur beings persist.

Meeting with Aphat to discuss this new development and to urge him to leash Ronan is of no use. He does not answer my calls. He's absent from the Andrak and has not been seen for some time. No doubt he's off to spend his time in one of the pleasure houses he favours while his empire descends into chaos.

By evening, I am nothing but simmering rage. Andrasar is in an upheaval and Seela travels further away from me.

She cannot remove her collar without my touch so I know her exact location. But the collar's range is limited and, inevitably, she will be lost to me forever.

How did she manage escape?

I check the location logs on her collar starting from when she left my quarters. Apparently she spent most of her day, even past curfew, in the infirmary.

I scowl at this. Did Eyin help her? Even though Eyin has never made it a secret that she does not support the enslavement of humans, she knows Seela is my fire's half. She wouldn't assist in her departure knowing Seela's importance to me.

So I make my way down to the infirmary to find out the truth.

"Of course I helped her escape," says Eyin without hesitation.

I've never been this furious with my sister in my life. It doesn't help that her tone is unconcerned as she confesses her treachery.

"Why would you do that? You could be imprisoned, Eyin."

"Are you going to tell Ronan and have me killed?" When I don't respond, she shrugs. "She wanted to leave so I helped."

"I can't believe you would do something like this. Especially when you know she's my—when you know what she is to me."

"I can't believe you would treat your fire's half so horrendously." She purses her lips. "You should have seen her. She looked so lost and alone and hurt. A strong spirit that's been broken. I don't know what you did, Theron, but regardless that you're my *rah* and I love you, you don't deserve her."

I run my hands through my hair sharply in frustration. Guilt and shame eating at me.

"You think I don't know that?" I say harshly. "Every single day she was here, every time I looked at her I was reminded of that fact."

"Then I did you both a service," she says. "She's out of sight and out of mind so you can go back to your old self. Not the one that *toha* and *kaha* tried to raise with decency and respect for others, but the one filled with hatred that Aphat and Ronan nurtured." Her tone is bitter, her features darkened with disappointment. "She can't be here, anyway.

Shihong's daughter, Xia, knows Seela saved your life and has told the other humans in the Andrak. She's now considered a traitor to her own kind."

When Eyin finishes speaking, I feel as battered and defeated as if she'd acquired the ability to shift and has beaten me to the ground.

"What do you want from me?" I rasp out. "What would you have me do?"

"Don't ask me that, Theron. You know exactly what you should do." She turns away from me. "I should get back to work."

She marches away from me to attend to a stirring patient.

I leave the infirmary, and for a while, I stand on one of the balconies and stare at the sprawl of Andrasar City.

In the distance, a plume of smoke curls toward the darkening sky. Those are common sights lately. A sign that yet another building is being destroyed by furious humans bent on fighting to the death for their freedom.

I resist at first, but I let myself entertain the thought of ceding to the humans' demands. I don't know my *toha*'s exact thoughts when he gave them refuge in Andrasar, but he must have believed it was the right choice to make.

He gave the humans lands within Andrasar to live and thrive on. He faced immediate disapproval from his people, yet he did not bend to their anger.

He and *kaha* were assassinated shortly after. Murdered as they slept.

Then Aphat rose to power, taking away my birthright as the Konai. Despite my suspicions that he took his brother's life, he convinced me that it was the humans who were responsible.

In the absence of the identity of my parents' murderer, it was easy to latch onto that explanation. It was easy to hate the humans because they were not like the Rur. It was easy to participate in their suffering in my misguided attempt at revenge.

In an old recording, my *toha* addressed Andrasar expressing his sadness that we as such strong beings could be reduced to the weakness of close-mindedness.

Seela said something similar to me when we first met.

Holding on to so much hate for beings you consider inferior only makes you weaker than them.

Hatred has robbed me of happiness and peace.

Hatred has made me weak.

Perhaps, it is time that I find strength.

Chapter Nineteen

Theron

Touching my implant, I search for Seela's location.

Miraculously, she has managed to make it out of the city and to the forest. She seems to have found the correct path that would lead her to Tarro.

Shifting into my dragon form, I fly toward the night sky. The cool air caresses my scales, the scent of the smoke wafting toward me. Whereas it might have taken Seela most of the day to get to the forest, it only takes me one *sen* at most.

Landing in the general area where the map last marked her, I continue the rest of the journey on foot. She would not have moved from where I last saw her. There's no moonlight to soften the pitch blackness,

Dragon's Captive

so to travel in the dark forest is asking for a quick death.

I pause when I pick up her scent. She is close, but she is hiding from me.

"Seela." I create a *safur* so she can see it's me and she shouldn't fear. Although, as far as she knows, I am still her enemy bent on keeping her captive. "Seela, I can find you if I wish but I would prefer if you revealed yourself willingly."

Silence.

Then the rustle of bushes as she steps into view.

Seeing her again is like seeing the sun expose itself after several long days of thunderstorms. I hadn't realized the weight I carried until the sight of her suddenly makes me light.

"I would prefer if you left me alone and flew back where you came from," she says.

"Not without you."

Distrust emanates from her, anger and hurt in her eyes. Her gaze dips briefly to survey my naked body before she bites her lip and glares at me.

"If you think I'll let you kidnap me again, you're sadly mistaken."

The words have barely left her mouth before she spins and bolts into the darkness. I cast the *safur* away and chase after her.

For a being whose vision is poor in absolute darkness, she's remarkably adept at evading the thick cluster of trees surrounding us.

Nevertheless, I catch up to her, snaring her by the waist. She's a wild animal in my arms, snarling, kicking, slapping, and squirming in an effort to get away from me. So I drag her to the floor and lean my weight down on top of her.

She continues to squirm in an attempt to get free. She can't see me but I have perfect vision in the darkness.

Her lips slacken as she breathes through her mouth. Her chest heaves against mine. This reminds me of that first night when I trapped her against a tree and felt my first temptation to kiss her.

That temptation surges within me again. I've had more than her kisses. I've had her body beneath mine just like this, my name on her lips, her heat and delicious scent driving me insane with need for her. Only her.

"I won't take you back to the Andrak if you don't want to return, Seela," I say. Then I add in a quieter voice. "I will even take you to Tarro if that is what you want. But there is something I need to tell you."

She stills. "What?"

"First, I will stand and help you to your feet," I say. "You will not try to run away from me. I want to take you somewhere."

"Why should I trust you?" she asks. "You're not above saying one thing and doing the next."

"Seela, in the time we've spent together, I'm sure you've learnt my ways. If I wanted to take you back to the Andrak, we would have been in the skies by now. You wouldn't be able to stop me."

"Boasting about how you can kidnap me if you wanted to isn't winning you any favours."

"I apologize."

Her eyebrows lift at that as if surprised I am capable of saying the words.

"Fine, then," she finally says. "I will go." I help her to stand and she grips my arms to balance herself in the darkness. "But as soon as we're finished with whatever you have to say, you're going to keep your word and take me to Tarro."

Even though her words irk me, I nod silently. Leading her back to where the first *safur* still eradicates the darkness, I warn her out of the way before I shift.

She looks at me in awe. My dragon is pleased that my fire's half appreciates its form and does not cower from it.

I lower my body and wait for her.

"You want me to ride you?" she asks in shock. "Isn't that forbidden in your culture?"

Would she prefer if I dangled her over the treetops like I did the last time I carried her? I cannot form words when in my dragon form, so I continue to wait for her as excitement chases away her distrust.

She approaches me. Meeting my gaze, she caresses my scales hesitantly. I am reminded of that first moment when we encountered each other. How she touched me this way before she saved my life.

By accepting that she is my fire's half, her touch arouses me now. I'm ready to shift into my primary form and take her when she lifts herself up onto my back. She inches her way up until she can wrap her hands around my neck, her heat pressing against me.

"Don't you dare drop me, Theron," she says, her voice soft with mild humour.

When I raise up in preparation to take flight, she lets out a startled exhale. She screams when I shove off the ground toward the sky.

As I fly, she makes sounds of wonder and I execute mild twirls to impress her. I'm intoxicated by the sound of her startled laughter, pleased that I can inspire other emotions in her beyond distrust and dislike.

The mountains loom ahead of us and before long, I set down on the flat surface that leads to the entrance of one of the dens

I shift and I reach for her hand. I'm already anticipating her pulling away from me, but she lets me guide her forward. A *safur* blooms in the palm of my hand, chasing away most of the darkness.

"This is a den," I tell her. "There are many of them within these mountains. Before the invention of cities and buildings, this is where the *rur draki* made their home."

"It seems like someone still lives here," she says, pointing at the furs that construct a bed.

"Yes, me. It belonged to my father. I come here every so often when I want to get away from the stress of work and the Andrak."

"I guess killing humans can be tiring work," she says, her tone cool as she slips her hand free from my grasp. All that lightness and humour as we flew has disappeared. "What is it that you wanted to talk about? I don't understand why you had to bring me all the way here to say it."

"You are my *asafura*, Seela," I say quietly. "Do you know what that means?"

She frowns as she picks her way through the literal translation. I'm surprised she doesn't know what it is since she has learned so much of Rur's culture from the Andrasari she lost.

"'One fire?'"

"It means *fire's half*," I explain. "Every *rur draki* has a mate who Kahafura has chosen specifically for them. They are half of a fire made whole and burning stronger when they have found and accepted their mate."

She shakes her head. "I am not a *rur draki* so obviously I can't be your fire's half."

"My dragon has a primitive mind, but the goddess has given it the ability to comprehend things beyond what I can in my primary form. It selects you as my *asafura*, Seela. It wants you as my mate." I drop my voice and draw closer to her. "*I* want you as my mate."

She has the look of someone who's suddenly been slapped with no explanation given by her attacker. There's a flicker of excitement and pleased amazement on her face before it's replaced by doubt, hurt and darkening anger.

"You threw me away, Theron," she says, her voice hollow as she drops her gaze. "For one moment you made me feel like I was everything you wanted. Then the next you rid yourself of me like I meant nothing to you.

Because I do mean nothing to you. I'm a human you can use and discard as you please. Just like the rest. Now here you are telling me I'm your—your *asafura and I'm supposed to believe you and jump into your arms?"

Her eyes shine with disbelief in the light from the *safur*. She shakes her head. "You captured me and enslaved me. You've killed a countless number of my people. You're a ruthless bastard whose only mission in life is destruction and I want nothing to do with you let alone be your mate."

I almost wince from the pain her words cause. It's worse because they are true. It's true that I don't deserve Seela. Perhaps I never will, but I would rather spend the rest of my years working to be better for her than not trying, than never having her in my life.

"I am sorry, Seela. Maybe it's too late to say it, but I am sorry for the things I've done to you, for my resistance to what was right." I want to touch her and hold her to me but I know she will not accept it. "Since that first night I met you, I wanted you. I grew up with a firm belief and here you were contradicting it entirely. That frightened me so I pushed you away. You must understand?"

Her only response is pursed lips and a steely gaze.

I exhale deeply. If talking won't get her to accept my sincerity, actions will have to do. When I move toward her, she immediately shuffles back and away from me. I catch her by her upper arms

"Stay still," I order her. Before she can give me the sarcastic retort I know is rising on her tongue, I touch the collar around her neck and disengage it. Then I fling it in some far, dark recess of the cave. "Never again will you or your people wear a collar."

She caresses her bare neck, her eyes round.

"What does that mean?"

"It means that I have stopped resisting. That I will work toward setting all humans free from slavery."

"And what about Aphat and Ronan? They'll object strongly to that."

"It will be the first hurdle, yes, but I will overcome it."

She is silent for some time before she looks away from me. I clench my fists at my sides in an effort to ward off the disappointment. I'm too late. I don't know why I'd expected she'd suddenly change her mind.

"Do you still want me to take you to Tarro?"

"Yes," she says quietly. Then she glances at me. "But not yet. I'm tired and want to rest first." She meets my gaze fully. "But if you don't want to wait, that's fine."

"I will wait." Not just tonight until she is rested and ready to leave me, but for as long as it takes before she finally forgives me, before she capitulates and accepts me as hers.

Chapter Twenty

Theron

"Why are you doing it? Why are you freeing the humans?"

A *safur*'s amber glow chases away the darkness to the corners of the den. Bare-skinned, Seela bathes in the den's heated pool.

From my vantage point on the furs, I can only see her slim shoulders, but if I were to draw closer, the clear water would reveal her nakedness entirely.

I cast my gaze to the jagged ceiling of the den above me. If I stare in Seela's direction any longer, the tenuous hold I have on my restraint not to drag her, wet and squealing, from the pool and take her would disappear.

"You showed me it's the right thing to do." I say. "I am tired of the strife within Andrasar. I would like to see it peaceful and prosperous again like it was when my father was the Konai."

She is silent for a moment.

"Thank you," she says quietly. "Whether or not you succeed, at least you're willing to try."

"There is one more reason," I say. "If humans are free, then there would be no need to hide that I want you."

Silence falls between us. Seconds become minutes. Then Seela rises from the pool, water sluicing down her naked, gorgeous form. Sitting up, I can't look away. Not especially as she approaches me.

Her gaze slides over me as she purses her lips.

"Eyin told me how she got her scar but how did you get yours?" she says softly.

Water drops cling to her skin and she glistens in the light. Her curls hang loose past her shoulders. They're limp from being wet, but some still curl, defiant like their owner.

I stare at her dusky pink lips, then her round, full breasts where the tips are dark buds against her brown skin. My gaze falls lower still over her smooth stomach, and then to that point between her legs where I would love to put my face, my tongue, my cock.

It's a struggle to remember her question when the sight of her steals my breath.

"From the same person. He punished and tortured me for several days because I almost killed him for hurting Eyin. My Shifted blood can't heal scars made from another Rur dragon."

Her features twists in fury. It pleases me that it's not directed toward me but it's on my behalf.

"Someday, Aphat is going to pay for all the things he's done."

Amusement tugs at my lips. "*Karma?*"

"Exactly." Then she frowns. "I think something is wrong with me. I wanted to hate you like I'm supposed to. I sat in the pool waiting for the hate but it never came."

"That does not mean something is wrong with you. It only means that you are more forgiving than the rest of us."

She stares at me silently, before she steps closer and caresses my face.

"Never again, Theron," she says. "Don't you ever hurt me again or you'll regret it. You know I don't make idle threats. I said I'd stab you that time and I made sure I did. *Twice.*"

Chuckling, I move to my knees and reach for her, slipping an arm around her body and hugging her close to me. Her skin is still wet from her bath but I don't mind. I press my lips to that smooth space between her breasts, kissing the supple curves of her flesh.

Her gasps fill me with satisfaction. I want to spend the rest my life hearing her make those tiny sounds. Her hands sift through my hair as I rove my hands down her soft thighs. Then I trail them back up to squeeze and grab her fleshy behind.

Her nipples are hard peaks. She shivers and moans whenever my lips get close to them. Her body gets taut in frustration, reaching for my lips on its own when I don't cover her nipples with my mouth.

I'm already painfully hard for this beautiful female. Not for the first time I'm overwhelmed that this exquisite creature desires me.

I thought I would be the one to break her, to drag her down into the darkness with me. But here I am on my knees before her with the hope that I can rise up to meet her in the light.

"Theron," she gasps when I finally suck her nipple into my mouth. Lapping and curling my tongue around the tip, I suck on her flesh. I slide my fingers slowly up the inside of her thigh, my fingers ghosting over her where she is already wet with arousal for me.

Her scent alone drives me crazy with lust. So soft and sweet just like her. I release her breast to press a kiss to her sternum, trailing a path of kisses over her stomach. Some day, if she will have me, our young will grow there.

Sitting back on my haunches, my face is level with her pelvis. I move my lips over the dip where her thighs meet her juncture as my fingers dip between her slightly parted legs. She is already so slick, her juices coating my fingers.

"Please...do it..." Seela squirms against my hand, begging for more of me with her body's movements too. I want more of her too. I incline my head and press my nose against her inhaling her divine scent.

My tongue snakes out, lapping at her in a quick dart and she jerks at this. That tiny sample I had is not enough. I need her spread out beneath me so that I can savour her.

Wrapping my arms around her, I pull her down so she can lie on her back on the furs. I cover her body with mine immediately, kissing her slowly even though my dragon demands I hasten to take her.

Our first encounter was quick, borne from desperation, from pent up frustration of wanting each other but being too afraid of the consequences. Tonight, I will explore Seela. I will make her mine for as long and as often as I can.

The silken wetness of her tongue curls against mine as we kiss. My hand grazes along her side from her ribcage down to her hip. When she works a hand between us to touch me, I groan into her mouth.

She jerks me, each stroke pulling moans from me. I break our kiss to pepper her jaw with kisses. Squirming, she tries to guide me into her. As much as I'm throbbing with desperation to bury myself inside her, I pull free from her grasp with a soft laugh.

"Not yet, greedy one."

She pouts and I suck her lower lip between my teeth before continuing on with what I'd intended. I kiss her chin, then her chest. As I secure one of her breasts in my palms, my mouth finds the other one.

She whimpers my name as I suckle her and pull on her nipples. Her sounds make me groan as I taste her. She is so responsive, unabashed in letting me know that she loves everything I do to her.

Releasing her breasts, I crawl down her body, placing feathery kisses to her skin on the way down. There's a shy look on her face as she spreads her legs open for me.

Even though I know I was not her first, she is still inexperienced. Fiery anger and jealousy rises inside me at the thought that another male has had her, but I dampen it. That doesn't matter. She is mine now. Always. There will be no other after me.

Her pussy glistens, inviting me forward. I drag my lips along the inside of her thighs and Seela raises her hips in expectation of my touch. She's so wet, her juices smear her thighs and I lap it up on the way to my prize.

My mouth hangs open over her, breathing hot air on her to torture her. She squirms, her hand flying to the back of my head in a silent, bossy demand I finish what I started. When I finally taste her for the first time we both groan in unison.

Fuck. She's so warm, so wet, her scent makes me dizzy how good it is. I have to keep holding down the beast inside me, keep telling myself to go slow, to savour her instead of devour her like my dragon commands.

I lick along the inside of her plump lips as I insert a finger into her heat. She is so tight, she grips my digit like a close sheath. When I had her on my cock that first night, I was on the brink of release just being inside her. Still, I add a second finger to her.

Dragon's Captive

"This," I say to her as I thrust my fingers into her, "is a promise of what's to come when I'm done making you come on my tongue, Seela."

"Oh..." she moans. Her fingers curl in my hair, fisting the strands. I find her tight little bud and cover it entirely with my mouth.

Sucking on it lightly, I slide my tongue back and forth on it. I am patient, enduring Seela's sharp tugs on my hair as she grinds her pussy against my mouth.

My cock throbs painfully, desperate to replace my fingers stroking her tight, wet heat. Yet I'm determined to give her what she needs, what she deserves and more from me.

Fucking her with my fingers, I continue to lap and suck incessantly on her. I squeeze her thigh with my free hand, holding her wide open so I can feast on her.

Soon, she's no longer just squirming. She bucks against me, her pleasure increasing. Her back curves away from the floor, her neck arching as she comes.

Her long moan and the way she squeezes my fingers is euphoric to me. When she's done trembling, I rise up and grasp her hips, and flip her over so that she's on her knees.

She lets out a little gasp of surprise when I embrace her from behind. I sit back on my haunches and she sits back against me.

Her legs spread open, her wet heat sits directly on my cock. She's so hungry for it she immediately begins sliding along my length, raising herself up so the head can push against her entrance.

I cup her full breast in one hand, my other delving between her legs to touch her exactly where I'm going to be shortly. I violate her with my fingers, my lips on her shoulder and the back of her neck. I bite her shoulder softly then caress where I bit with my tongue.

"Theron," she begs, "Please... please, stop making me wait..."

Goddess above there's no sweeter sound than my fire's half begging for my cock.

My hand on her shoulder, I push her down so she's on all fours in front of me. I position myself behind her, rubbing my shaft along her dripping wetness.

Eagerness to be inside her builds in me, but I bend over to drop kisses on her smooth back. Reaching around to fondle her full breasts, I slide them down her sides.

Touching Seela alone brings me almost as much satisfaction as fucking her.

My fingers dig into her hip while I guide myself into her heat. She moans and trembles as I press into her. Grabbing both of her hips, I surge into her into her deep and full, rocking her forward.

A choked gasp escapes her and her tight sheath steals a pained groan from me. I've wanted to be inside her for so long that I'm almost reluctant to move for fear the next stroke might be my undoing.

Seela squirms, already impatient for more, and I have to comply with the wishes of my mate. I thrust into her, slow at first to regain control of myself. She's such a tiny creature in comparison to me. When I look down between us where my cock slides into her, I'm reminded how much bigger I am to her. My worry that I'm hurting her is swept away when Seela rocks back against me in a quest for a harder fucking.

So I tangle my fingers in her lovely curls and give her what she wants. I drive into her, and she takes everything I give to her with moans of pleasure. Her back bows as she comes again, her body taut as she pants for air. She spasms around me, tighter than ever and I share her groans.

Mark her as yours.

I continue to thrust into her as I bend over her, my chest pressed against her back.

"Do you accept me as yours, Seela?" I growl in her ear. "Do you accept me as your fire's half?"

"Yes, Theron... you're mine...you're my fire's half..." she pants without hesitation. "Just like I am yours."

Her acceptance fills me with triumph and joy, makes the beast inside me roar victorious. My lips part, my teeth lengthening into fangs. The tips prick her flesh before they sink fully into the claiming bite.

She cries out in pain but her cry rapidly dissolves into a long moan. I soothe the mark with my tongue as I release her. She shivers violently, another climax accosting her.

She grips me so tightly that she pulls me to my finish. My seed shoots from me with such intensity that my vision darkens and I nearly collapse on top of her.

Breathing heavily, we sink to the furs in blissful satisfaction.

I hold my mate against me, relishing the soft kisses she presses to my throat.

I was incomplete when I did not know of her existence.

Now that she is here with me, I am made whole.

Chapter Twenty-One

Seela

Theron wakes me.

Daylight streams into the entrance of the den, revealing a pinched look of anger and worry on his handsome features.

"You need to get dressed quickly," he says as I blink to keep my eyes open. I am still pleasantly exhausted from what we did most of the night before. "Ronan is near."

That wakes me up.

"Maybe he's just passing by," I say, but I hurry to dress anyway.

"I doubt it."

Finally, worry catches up to me.

"How does he know we're here?"

Dragon's Captive

Theron glances in the direction he threw my collar last night.

"He must have found the collar's id from the database and hunted you down using the tracker."

But why is he hunting me? Whatever the reason, the end result won't be good for me.

"I will not let him take you," says Theron as he grabs my hand and leads me out of the den.

We are stopped in our tracks when three *draki* lands before us. It's the first time I've ever been this close to so many dragons and the sight is daunting.

They all look like dark, gigantic monsters covered in scales, but every *rur draki* has unique patterns differentiating themselves from each other.

I recognize Ronan's dragon form right away. His scales aren't black but deep grey. And he looks the most menacing of the three.

As if to solidify my guess, he shifts into his primary form. The other two remain as they are in their dragon form like monstrous guards.

"I am glad you are here, Theron," he says, a dark smile curving his lips. "I'm afraid I bring bad news. Last night, the Konai was found dead. Medics say he's been dead for a few days."

Theron's features mirrors my own surprise. As much as there is no sadness in the news, there is no joy either.

"Then why are you here and not searching for his murderer?"

"I have found her already," Ronan says with sinister glee. "The spawn of that human I executed was recorded via her collar plotting the crime. You and I were also her targets."

Xia killed Aphat? I find it hard to believe even though I know how much Xia hated him. My skin prickles with dread as Ronan's gaze lands on me.

"This vermin to whom you have taken an unnatural and disgusting fancy was overheard on the recording encouraging the murderer."

Immediately, I realize what he's talking about. That last conversation I had with Xia before she stormed off. How she threatened to kill those she felt had done her an injustice.

At the time, she was angry and hurt. People tend to say things or make outlandish threats and promises they don't mean when they're in such emotional state. That doesn't mean they intended to hold true to their words.

Besides, Ronan is a known liar. He killed Shihong and imprisoned the rest of us under false charges. Now he's twisting my words. Livid, I am shaking. I open my mouth, ready to call him what he is, but Theron speaks first.

"The next time you refer to my fire's half in such an insulting manner will be your last, Ronan," says Theron coldly and Ronan's features twist in disgust. "You speak lies. Seela does not encourage others to take lives. So if you are lying about this, then I question the rest of what you've said." He steps forward, making sure to keep me from Ronan's direct reach. "Did you kill Aphat?" I can't see his face, but there's a deadliness to his voice.

He focuses his baleful gaze on Theron in silence. If he killed Aphat, he would never admit.

"I suppose there's no point in hiding anymore since you won't be leaving here alive," he says. "Of course it was I who killed Aphat. And it was I who had you attacked in the forest that day."

"Why, Ronan?" Theron asks his tone equally betrayed and furious. "I shared no love for Aphat, but he was your friend. I was your friend. Why did you turn against us?"

"Because you all disappointed me," Ronan says. "I thought you would become the Konai I could serve. Your *toha* invited pests into our great region and your *okan* only cared about the benefits of being a Konai. But you... you cared about Andrasar as a Konai should. Unfortunately, you are Dohar's son. His weakness lived on inside of you despite my attempts to teach you strength." He sneers. "You grew complacent in your duties, allowing the humans to survive among us. Then you spared their lives. And now you claim one as your mate." He shakes his head in disgust. "No Visclaud is worthy of the title of Konai. Only I can make Andrasar great again."

"I will die before I let Andrasar fall prey to your treacherous, war-mongering hands."

Ronan laughs evilly. "Truly like father, like son. Dohar said the same before I took his and your *kaha*'s useless lives."

With a snarl, Theron shifts and charges at Ronan, breathing fire.

As Ronan returns to his dragon form and retaliates, the other two *draki* join in on the fight. It's an uneven match, three against one.

I want to help Theron in some way, but what can I do when even their tails are larger than me? So I'm forced to retreat to the inside of the den.

I look on in terror as the Andrasari male who has become important to me battles against three of his kind.

My heart pounds as violently as the ground shakes. Theron bites the neck of one *draki*, tearing through its toughened scales, severing a significant portion of its flesh.

Copious amounts of dark blood sprays everywhere. It's a horrifying sight, the *draki*'s pained howl making my blood curdle. It returns to its primary form, the wound even more gruesome as the Andrasari male falls dead to the ground.

Spreading his wings, Theron launches into the air and the remaining two pursue him.

He does not fly far. He darts away abruptly, circling to grab hold of the *draki* that's closest so he could breathe fire in its face and tear open its chest with his vicious claws.

As that second *draki* falls from the sky in his primary form, the third retreats from Theron. It dives toward where I stand.

It's Ronan and he's coming for me.

But Theron catches him first, slamming into him so they both crash toward the ground near the den's entrance. I lose my balance and fall backward from the force of the impact. The floor is sunk where they land, fissures expanding outward.

The fight might be evenly matched now but Ronan seems as strong as Theron. They tussle, swiping and clawing at the each other.

When he clamps his teeth on Theron's neck, I don't think. Logic vanishes. This monster is ready to end the life of my Andrasari and I won't let it. I shove to my feet and pick up a hefty rock nearby, flinging it at him to distract him.

He immediately raises his head and belts a wave of fire in my direction.

I scream and throw myself to the ground, scrambling away as fast as I can into the den's depths. The fire misses me, but the heat is so intense I'm drenched in sweat.

A howl sounds and my heart lurches into my throat. I'm too far into the den to see what has happened, but fury and pain is an awful, leaden mix in my chest at the thought that my help was in vain, that Ronan still killed Theron.

Uncaring that Ronan will kill me next, I race out of the den.

But where there were two *draki*, there are now two Andrasari males in their primary form. Ronan lays dead on the ground, a sickening sight as most of his insides are outside his body. He must have perished because of that brief moment of inattention when he tried to burn me alive.

Theron, weak and breathing hard, stands over Ronan. Overwhelmed with joy, I reach for him. He encompasses me in a possessive grip and I hold him against me without care that he's covered in blood and gore.

He's mine.

He's alive.

That's all that matters.

Chapter Twenty-Two

Seela

In the wake of Aphat's death, Theron becomes the new Konai of Andrasar.

And true to the promise he made to me that night in the den, he frees all humans from slavery.

Surprisingly, many Andrasari support the decision. They are happy to escape the remnants of Aphat's violent reign and foster peace in their region.

Of course, there are still those who believe that humans and Rur beings should not coexist. They are now the few. Those who continue to exhibit hostility and violence toward humans are caught and imprisoned.

As much as the freedom from slavery is a good thing, it leaves Andrasar in temporary disarray.

Dragon's Captive

While some humans remain in their positions, many leave gaps in the workforce as they move to form communities in the lands Theron award them.

Others, like Xia, decide to leave Andrasar to explore the rest of Rur.

"Where will you go?" I ask her. It has taken some time, because Xia is not one who forgives easily, but she and I have reconciled. She stands with me on the balcony before the doors of the home Theron and I share.

"I don't know." She shifts her bag's strap on her shoulder. "Tarro, Naveth, Yohai... maybe even Seca. As long as it's not here."

"I heard Seca is nothing but ice," I say with a small smile.

"Maybe I'll freeze to death," she says, staring out over the city surrounding us. "That's what I deserve."

My smile disappears. Just as Xia does not forgive others easily, she also doesn't forgive herself for her Shihong's death.

"Be safe on your journey, Xia," I say. I raise my hands to hug her but I pause and drop them. We might have reconciled, but there's still tension between us. I believe it stems from the fact that I am in a relationship with Theron. She still despises him.

She looks at me for some time. Long enough to make me fidget. Then, to my surprise, she pulls me into her arms in a full hug.

"I'm sorry, Seela," she whispers. "I don't think you are a traitor. I will never have the sort of strength like you do to save someone who wanted me dead." When she pulls away, she dashes a hand across her eyes to wipe away her tears. "If it were me who found Theron in the forest that day, we would have all still been wearing collars."

"Don't underestimate yourself, Xia. You are strong."

"I'm not." She shakes her head, then she smiles as she backs away from me in preparation to leave. "But maybe I'll grow up someday and become just like you, Konai sa of Andrasar."

Heat floods my face. "That's not my title."

With a laugh and a wave, she leaves me by myself on the balcony.

I fold my arms around myself against the slight chill. The view of the city below brings me peace. I'm startled when a pair of strong arms surround me, batting away the cold from me effortlessly.

"It could be," Theron says, the rumble of his voice vibrating against my back, his lips moving against my ear. I shiver, but not because I'm cold. He knows this

Dragon's Captive

is my weakness. When he holds me, his voice low and silken in my ear. I immediately feel safe and content and aroused.

"What could be?" I ask.

"The title of Konai sa could be yours if you wished it."

Those words make me instantly alert. I turn in his arms to face him, my heart rate speeding up. I've been his mate for nearly a hundred *detar* now learning as much about him as he does about me.

Every day, every moment I spend with him, every instance his hands and lips pleasure me make me fall harder and deeper in love with him. The first time we met, this Andrasari male threatened my life.

We were enemies willing to hurt each other for preservation. That seems so long ago. Now, he showers me with endless love and devotion.

"Are you asking me to marry you, Theron?"

He tries to hide it, but I see the vulnerable look on his face anyway.

"Only if your answer is yes and nothing else."

"You're arrogant even in marriage proposals."

I say no more, delighting in the scowl darkening his features as he waits. When I was his *zevyet* he would have threatened me for refusing to answer him. He isn't my *zevyena* anymore. He is my mate who respects me and never fails to show me I am of extraordinary value to him.

"Well?"

"Well, what?"

"What is your answer?" Without warning, his hand drops from around me and delves under my dress. His fingers skim the inside of my thigh before they rub me where I'm already damp. "Or perhaps you need some convincing?"

"Convincing is a great idea," I say breathlessly when his fingers push aside my underwear and slips inside my wet heat.

His fingers buried inside me, stroking me, Theron brushes his lips against mine.

"Will you marry me, Seela?" he asks softly.

"Yes," I gasp out when his thumb circles me. "Yes, I'll marry you."

I feel his triumphant smirk against my lips as he withdraws his fingers and lifts me into his arms.

"Then with this good action it's time you received your deserved reward."

Epilogue

Seela

I finally make it to Tarro one *enu* later.

However, I'm not by myself. I have my fire's half with me.

Theron and I walk along a brightly lit street crowded with people. It's mostly Rur beings, but some humans mill about too. Slave collars aren't wrapped around their necks anymore, and their faces are bright with smiles.

Booths hosting games or selling food and other gifts populate either side of the street. Lively music and excited voices fill the air.

"This is the *Ranasfura* Festival," Theron explains. "*Great mountain of fire*. Ranas is Rur's largest

Dragon's Captive

volcano. Many *draki* from all over the planet come to celebrate its eruption."

"Call me crazy but a volcanic eruption doesn't sound like an event one should celebrate."

"Ah, then perhaps I should cancel my plans to take you right over Ranas' entrance to witness the eruption closely?" He chuckles at my horrified face. "There is nothing to fear. The lava pours into the sea. The *draki* believe the heated waters strengthen them so they bathe in it."

His hand on the small of my back he guides me to a booth and buys me a cold sweet treat.

"Why are you smiling?" Theron asks.

"Because I just realized something." I lick my lips to gather up the sweet moisture from the treat. "Aside from his arrogance and bossiness, my husband has a romantic side too." I smirk at him. "Today's the anniversary of the day we met."

He raises an eyebrow, feigning nonchalance.

"It is? What a coincidence."

"You and I both know it isn't."

His lips curve in amusement as he takes my hand, sliding his fingers between mine. I press my lips together, a quivery sensation in my belly from his touch. I'm always amazed how easily Theron can make me want him. He makes me warm and damp between my thighs from a half-lidded glance, or his fingers against my skin, or his lips moving against my earlobe as his silken voice caresses me.

"Come," he says when I've finished my treat. "I know the best view for you to see Ranas breathe fire without the fumes harming you."

He shifts into his dragon form, large, impressive and drawing everyone's attention. He waits for me to climb on top of him and I do so with my face and ears burning. It's still awkward for me to ride him in public because it's been forbidden in Andrasar for so long. Theron doesn't care. He says it brings him joy to have his mate fly with him. It makes me happy too. I will never be able to sprout wings and fly, but this is a great alternative.

Wrapping my arms around his neck, I squeal a little as he takes off for the sky. I don't think I'll ever get over that dropping sensation in the pit of my stomach as Theron shoots up into the air.

He pumps his wings a few times then spreads them fully as we soar over the tops of buildings and trees. Soon, we land on a cliff's edge, a thick cluster of trees behind it. Theron returns to his primary form completely naked. I try to be inconspicuous in my usual gawking at his muscular frame.

The scars on his flesh no longer anger me as much as they used to. That awful period of his life is completely over, especially since the Andrasari who gave them to him has been dead for some time.

Theron's front is nothing but defined flesh, his arms thick and visibly hard. The half-circle scales on his skin are as golden as his eyes.

Goddess above, there are days when I can't believe this handsome, powerful Andrasari male is *mine*.

Theron leads me to a tree with a broad trunk and branches spread wide. He sits, tugging me with him to the floor and between his legs. As he wraps his arms around me and pulls me close, I'm conscious of his cock right against the small of my back.

"There," he says, pointing at the huge, dark mountain looming in the distance. A bright orange glow blooms at its top. Several *draki* circle it in various directions.

"They look eager."

"Some prefer to touch the lava itself and not wait for it to fall into the sea."

"Why do I get the sense that you're among these 'some'?"

He laughs. "That's because you know me too well."

The orange bloom deepens into a violent red as the eruption unfolds. The *draki* surrounding Ranas breathe fire and swoop toward the lava being spit free. A thick plume of smoke rises out of the open top and mist forms where the lava spills into the sea.

It's a captivating sight, and all my attention is focused on it until Theron moves his hand to my thigh.

His touch is innocent at first. A gentle, idle rub over the material of my dress. Then his hand slips to the edge of my dress. His fingers trail from my knee along the inside of my thigh. There's absolutely no question as to what that hard rigid thing pressing against my back could be as his fingers inch closer to where I need him the most.

"I should have known you didn't just bring me up here for the view," I say.

"Are you accusing your Konai of hidden motives? Others are punished severely for less crimes."

"If the crown fits, let him wear it."

Theron's questing fingers find me and I gasp, lifting my hips to press firmer against his touch.

"You're naked under your dress, Konai sa," he says against my ear as he trails his fingers along my slit. "Maybe you are the one with ulterior motives."

Pressing his lips to my neck, his tongue snakes out, licking me once before sucking the skin there. The damp heat makes me shiver, more so when the pads of his fingers center on my swollen nub and he rubs me in patient, insistent circles.

"Theron..." I moan. Squirming, I dig into the hard earth on either side of us. Theron palms my breast with his free hand over my dress. He yanks at the top, pulling it down to reveal my soft flesh to his rough, greedy hand.

He smooths a thumb over the pebbled tip, flicking it and mimicking the action on my nub. His length presses into my back, unmistakably large and rigid. I want it in me, stretching me more than anything. My desperation must be evident because Theron spears me with his fingers. He slips his hand up from my breast to my chin, twisting my face so he can cover my mouth with his.

He kisses me fiercely, greedily. His tongue sweeping into my mouth and claiming mine. He thrusts his fingers into me, quick and even, his digits expertly finding that pleasurable spot inside me that makes me come undone. He sucks my tongue into his mouth and swallows my whimper, groaning in satisfaction as my walls constrict his digits.

He holds me to him as my shivering lessens and I spin to climb on top of him. I'm drenched already and I make sure he feels what he's done to me by sliding my wetness against his length as I sit on him.

Cupping his face into my hands, I kiss him again.

"I love you," I say softly.

"I love you, Seela," he says in return, then he groans as I sink onto him.

It's not something we say to each other often. We prefer to show it to each other. Like in this moment when our bodies are joined together, and he holds me so tightly against him in his strong arms that I know he never wants to let me go.

Theron pulls the top of my dress down to my stomach, revealing me to his appreciative gaze and hungry lips. Cupping my bottom, he moves me on him as he dips his head to claim my breasts in his mouth. I cling to his shoulders, my fingernails sinking into his flesh as his hard length thrusts into me.

We've made love countless times since we've accepted each other as a mate, but every instance still feels as thrilling and fresh as that first night he took me on his floor. I rove my fingers though his hair, pressing his face to my chest. I want him to have all of me just like he gives me all of him as he fills me.

Theron moves me to lie on the ground, covering my body with his. He groans as he continues to thrust into me, peppering my face with kisses. He latches onto that spot on my neck where he gave me the claiming bite. Every time he touches or kisses me there, intense pleasure sweeps through me. It does so now as his tongue laps against it.

When I come, it's explosive and makes me scream as loud as the dragons roaring over Ranas. Theron groans my name too, his cock like steel inside me as his seed shoots from him into me. It's my hope that someday it will take root and I will give him a young *drakila*.

I hold him to me as we recover and he nuzzles my neck.

"I did remember," he says, his voice low.

He lifts his head, his golden eyes shining with so much love it stops my breath. There once was a time when he looked at me differently. There once was a time so long ago when he was my worst enemy.

But no longer.

He is my first and my only love.

"What did you remember?" I ask, dragging a finger over his lips. He is still inside me and I squeeze him in anticipation as I feel him thickening.

"That today is the day we first met one *enu* ago." He bends his head, feathering a kiss on my lips as he gives a gentle thrust into me that makes me gasp. "I will never forget the day that I was blessed with you."

***

Thank you for reading Dragon's Captive.

Please take a moment to leave an opinion about this book. Readers rely on reviews and your opinion can help others decide on future purchases. Make your vote count!

Sign up to Shea's list for new release alerts
http://www.sheamalloy.com/newsletter

Glossary

Asafura: fire's half; the fated mate of a Rur being

Draki: dragon

Rur draki: Rur dragon

Kahafura: mother of fire and goddess of Rur; a deity

Konai: High Prince; the leader of a region in Rur

Konai sa: High Princess

Ta Konai: My Prince; a formal/respectful way to address a Konai

Nai: Prince

Nai sa: Princess

Kaha: mother

Toha: father

Niha: son

Nihasa: daughter

Rahsa: sister

Rah: brother

Okan: uncle

Safur: a ball of light and warmth formed from the energy source of a Rur being

Zevyet: slave

Zevyena: slave master(s) or master(s)

Time on Rur

Enu(r): year(s)

Deta(r): day(s)

Sen: hour(s)

28 sen in 1 deta

402 detar in 1 enu

There are no weeks or months on Rur.

Shea Malloy

Shea Malloy writes steamy, action-packed stories. Her books feature strong, protective men, and brave, feisty women of all colours finding love in the midst of danger and adventure.

She lives in Canada with her husband and two adorable cats. When she's not reading or writing, she nerds it up in web development for fun.

Books by Shea Malloy
http://www.sheamalloy.com

Printed in the USA
CPSIA information can be obtained
at www.ICGtesting.com
LVHW091458190924
791500LV00051B/522